"Cesi Da[...] trip around, through, and within the heart. These short journeys into the emotions of those who love and those who do not add to our understanding of what love is and what love isn't. When you laugh, cry, and sigh with recognition, you will be reminded that you are not only a witness to, but also a participant in the emotional life of all those around you. I hope you will enjoy these jump-starts to the heart as much as I did."

—Celeste Rita Baker, World Fantasy Award Winner, author of *Back, Belly and Side* celesteritabaker.com

"Cesi Davidson's newest book of short plays is at the same time revolutionary and hilarious in its content and delivery. Appropriately, the first play is titled "Juicy," and this book has so much sweet, liquid fun within. From the beginning, the reader experiences a trickle of exquisite sensuality running through each page. There is an emboldened message of contented sexuality in many of the pieces that I, as a woman, felt incredibly grateful to tune in to. Cesi gives a gift to those of us with female bodies—and that gift is permission to feel good, whatever it looks like, and to research what could feel even better! Like Chauncey, the husband whose wife keeps watch over his every move, the characters in these plays refuse to be imprisoned. They have reached a turning point, and we watch, delighted, as change washes over everyone like a gigantic, juicy wave."

—Kim Chinh, actor, screenwriter, playwright, author of "Reclaiming Vietnam" kimchinh.com

"The writing smoothly creates images, colors, and situations that lead the reader into the different immersed situations. Within the landscape of these various situation life issues, for example, humanity, identity, roles, expectations, and the rainbow of emotions, etc. are being done without going into darkness. In between the plays the prose capsulized a prospective of the former that was out of plain sight. It was like a cleansing of the palate for the next situation.

"Personally, the reading experience felt like a nice girl's erotic sexual liberation written in a beautiful picturesque code for those who can hear, see, and feel her liberation and emotions within the stories.

"Entertaining reading."

—Aduke Mickey Davidson, Senior Choreographer and Educator for "The Makanda Project," "Jazz Power Initiative," and Mickey D & Friends Dance/Music Co.

"Once again I was entertained, moved, and shocked by Cesi's expansive imagination in this third collection of inventive and delightful short plays. Give yourself to Cesi's words, and you'll experience the true essence of love with plenty of laughter inside the rich world in which all beings are sentient, intelligent, and funny."

—Rachel Lu (Actor, Elite Match)

Bilabials

Conversation Pieces

A Small Paperback Series from Aqueduct Press
Subscriptions available: www.aqueductpress.com

About the Aqueduct Press
Conversation Pieces Series

The feminist engaged with sf is passionately interested in challenging the way things are, passionately determined to understand how everything works. It is my constant sense of our feminist-sf present as a grand conversation that enables me to trace its existence into the past and from there see its trajectory extending into our future. A genealogy for feminist sf would not constitute a chart depicting direct lineages but would offer us an ever-shifting, fluid mosaic, the individual tiles of which we will probably only ever partially access. What could be more in the spirit of feminist sf than to conceptualize a genealogy that explicitly manifests our own communities across not only space but also time?

Aqueduct's small paperback series, Conversation Pieces, aims to both document and facilitate the "grand conversation." The Conversation Pieces series presents a wide variety of texts, including short fiction (which may not always be sf and may not necessarily even be feminist), essays, speeches, manifestoes, poetry, interviews, correspondence, and group discussions. Many of the texts are reprinted material, but some are new. The grand conversation reaches at least as far back as Mary Shelley and extends, in our speculations and visions, into the continually created future. In Jonathan Goldberg's words, "To look forward to the history that will be, one must look at and retell the history that has been told." And that is what Conversation Pieces is all about.

L. Timmel Duchamp

Jonathan Goldberg, "The History That Will Be" in Louise Fradenburg and Carla Freccero, eds., *Premodern Sexualities* (New York and London: Routledge, 1996)

Conversation Pieces
Volume 84

Bilabials

Short Plays to Nourish
the Mind & Soul

by
Cesi Davidson

Published by Aqueduct Press
PO Box 95787
Seattle, WA 98145-2787
www.aqueductpress.com

For information on licensing rights for production of a
play in this collection contact the author directly:
cesidavidson@gmail.com

ISBN: 978-1-61976-228-2

Cover courtesy Michal Ammar
Cover background, © Can Stock Photo / realcg
Interior color photographs of flowers
courtesy Cesi Davidson

Original Block Print of Mary Shelley by Justin Kempton:
www.writersmugs.com

Printed in the USA by Applied Digital Imaging

For Aunt Kitty and Uncle Louie

Bilabials require two lips

Contents

Foreword

She's a Wonder

Cesi Davidson is a wonder. There's no other way to describe her consistently prolific invention, the fertility of her imagination, or the stunning boldness with which she deploys it in this, her most recent exposition of short plays and prose titled *Bilabials*. According to Davidson, *Bilabials* is meant "to Nourish the Mind and Soul"; it certainly accomplishes that, and so much more. It astonishes.

I first met Cesi Davidson lifetimes ago. Friendships are sometimes like that.

We were at Woody King Jr.'s New Federal Theater for an evening playwriting workshop. I arrived late and struggled to find a seat at the table. Eight writers were seated ready with their scripts on the table. The sagging metal chairs made balance difficult. The table didn't easily accommodate adult sized bodies. Its cafeteria-style edges were blunted by generations of St. Augustine's catechism students, most of them young, gifted, and Black. In the sanctuary, you could see the old "Slave Gallery" that still hung over congregational activity. Woody King had a small suite of offices behind the sanctuary, and from there, he ushered us into the world of theater.

Neither the physical discomfort nor challenging late night hours stopped Cesi's prolific outpouring. Week after week, she wrote play after play, sometimes bringing two or three startling new works in an evening. She listened to feedback, with regal composure and genuine

1

studiousness. She followed her north star until the quality, often coveted, but rarely understood, became her trademark. She's authentic as hell.

Davidson's collected works span three volumes, *Fricatives*, *Articulation*, and this new edition, *Bilabials*, comprising a theatrical opus. Each of the small works contains elements of the epic as well as the personal. In *Bilabials*, she treads fearlessly through love and loss, displacement, alienation, grief, sexuality, and we go with her to the depths and the summit of human experience. Her willingness to show a character's complexity and contradictions, their good and bad days, their nice, their ugly, gives us a window into Black women's lives and a healing bridge to universal truths.

It is tempting to compare Davidson's theater to that of Ionesco, Strindberg, Genet, or Cocteau. Like them, Davidson confronts a world where human connection is tenuous, where chaos and violence are imminent, a world where we must use language as a sword to cut through the noise, the lies, and the fears we hide from one another. Her short plays are epigrammatic in nature; they condense lifetimes of experience into brief encounters and present large, existential questions in spare, elegant dialogue. With skillful brevity, she constructs not just a mirror to hold up to our lives, but a many-sided prism through which we may ponder the nature of our reality. Deceptively simple at first glance, the plays are all highly organized and full of complexity that challenge and excite the reader or theatergoer.

And then, there is the wonder of humor. Davidson's collected works contain satirically humorous characters in situations that lay bare hypocrisy and deflate pomposity. In our time of cultural malaise, Cesi Davidson's works provide an antidote to mediocrity and spur us towards a more creative future.

It's been a long time since we sat in wobbly chairs and read our scripts at tables with bent edges. But I always knew Cesi Davidson would stand among the extraordinary dramatists of our day. She is part of a continuum, a tradition of fearless and truthful creators. Like Bessie Smith's "Ma Rainey," like Arthur Mitchell's Dance Theater of Harlem, Jacob Lawrence's Migration Series, and Ntozake Shange *For Colored Girls Who Have Considered Suicide/When the Rainbow Is Enuf*, she's here, and she's bringin' it.

> Thea Martinez
> Author of numerous choreopoems;
> performing with the Nuyorican Cafe Theater,
> and contributed choreography to the original
> production of *For Colored Girls* at Woody
> King's New Federal Theatre

Preface

Welcome to my bouquet of plays and prose. In short, welcome to my words. Some related. Some, not so much. All have something to say as they give voice through the experience of Fem. And like a bouquet, you can enjoy each flower for its individuality. You can also consider how the individuality adds to the composition of the whole arrangement.

I hold these flowers in my arms and offer them to you. Read them in any order that suits your "Fem Fancy" or inquisitive "Fem Curiosity." Stand up, sit down, squat, lie down, roll over, step into, or jump through the words. From my body to yours, with love. Some stems have thorns. Watch out or not. You may bleed. Some have lingering beautiful aromas. Perhaps, resonating with your own scents. Some stink profusely. That's life. Everything beautiful isn't beautiful. But I can assure you, that there will be petals.

As a child I loved the beauty of flowers while being afraid of them. Love them. They die. Drying their flower bodies never felt the same. Then growing into "woomanhood," I learned that there is never a beginning, or an end. Joy is infinite and filled with changes. The experience of being human is that nothing changes unless it changes. Change means we are spiritually alive, and transforming.

The final arrangement of this book bouquet is up to you. You're also invited to compost: renew, regenerate, restore.

Peace and Love, Cesi
May 2022

Rose was gorgeous

She had one physical eye

Four fingers on each hand

Her cleft lips had been poorly repaired with surgery

Her left arm was shorter than the right

She wrote poetry and signed contracts with her left hand

Her legs reached from the hip sockets to the knees

Her genital worked perfectly

Rose knew that a woman is responsible for her own joy and possibilities

She was boundless

Rose was a self-loving woman

Juicy

Characters

Karen: Woman in her early thirties

Lee: Man in his late thirties

Setting

Springtime. A park bench. New York City.

(Lights Rise)

LEE: (Looking straight ahead) Lovely day.

KAREN: (Looking straight ahead) Yes it is…a lovely day.

LEE: Expect rain?

KAREN: No. You?

LEE: No. A little cloudy.

KAREN: Yes, just a little. Could be rain. James took his trench coat to work.

LEE: Yes, could be.

KAREN: What?

LEE: Rain

KAREN: Could be… How's your Mom?

LEE: Oh, Oh, Mom's great! She had her annual physical. Good heart, lungs, stamina, everything. Doctor says, physically she could live for years and years. Still a beautiful woman. We had dinner together. I almost thought she recognized me. She looked at me. Didn't say anything. But she looked at me. But then again, she seemed to be doing more looking at everybody yesterday. Last month she wasn't looking at all, just rocking back and forth. If it was possible to look inside yourself, that's what she was doing. I remember, in January when she was looking all the time, she had a special look for me. I know it was special for me. I know it was. She looked at my eyes, and it seemed like she was trying to hold on to me with her eyes. She didn't do that with anyone else. I think she wanted to say my name because her jaw dropped open wide like she was saying /l/ for "Lee," but no sound came out. I thought that maybe by springtime she would be saying more. It's still spring, it's still possible.

KAREN: I'm sure it's possible Lee.

LEE: The Good Shepherd Home accepted her. I'm taking her on Tuesday. I'm so lucky. So lucky. They're clean. The nurses are licensed, and most of them were nice when I visited.

KAREN: People usually have a hard time taking care of their family…when you know…they stop remembering so well.

LEE: I remember, just before the Christmas holiday Mom left all the burners turned on and left the house. She didn't have her coat. Went out in her housedress and her slippers. The super found her sitting on the curb at the taxi stand across from our building. She had forgotten where she lived. After that I knew I couldn't leave her alone in the apartment any more. Even with neighbors looking in and checking on her it just wasn't safe.

LEE: (Hesitation and despair in his voice) I sold her acres in Alabama to make a down payment on the nursing home. The insurance hasn't kicked in yet. Did you know old people can't have assets to get the long-term government insurance? Doesn't matter I guess. She doesn't remember Alabama or anything else.

KAREN: You did what you had to do.

> (Lee and Karen look at each other. They penetrate each other with their eyes. Movement in unison. Lee takes two plums from a paper bag. He holds them with a single cupped hand with parted legs next to his genitals. Karen takes plums from her paper bag. She holds one in each hand next to the nipples of her breasts. Then in unison they place the fruit on the park table in front of them.)

LEE: I always wash my hands before I eat plums. A lot of men don't do that you know. I think it's respectful.

KAREN: Women appreciate when a man washes his hands first. I know I do.

LEE: (Points to one of the plums on the table) That one is a Goldenrod Plum.

KAREN: I've sucked on other types of rods before but never a Goldenrod.

LEE: It has firm flesh and a small pit inside.

KAREN: Pits are important. I like to have my pit touched. Sometimes a firm fleshy plum has a soft, chewy pit.

LEE: When the pit is soft, I chew on it and swallow it.

KAREN: (Indicating one of the plums on the table) I enjoy sucking.

There are dry plums, and there are juicy plums. I can tell if the plum is juicy when I look at the outside. I hold the plum in the palm of my hand, and I make just a little nip in the flesh. Just enough for the juice to start dripping out. Then I start to suck. I let it drip on my face. Suck and drip, suck and drip, suck and drip, swallow.

LEE & KAREN: (Orgasmic moment) JUICY

LEE: Do you stroke the flesh while you suck?

KAREN: Yeah Baby.

LEE: Do you hold on to the flesh tight?

KAREN: I make magic with my mouth. Nip, suck, drip, stroke, nip, suck, drip, stroke, and pull.

LEE: JUICY

KAREN: When I finish...I don't like it when I'm still hungry!

LEE: You already told me how you feel about your pits. Big Daddy can take care of some pits.

KAREN: Most men don't know how to take care of pits, and the whole experience just becomes so unpleasant!

LEE: I have magic fingers. (Indicates one of the plums on the table) See that one. I would work the front and the back. It has a beautiful little stem. Most men neglect the stem.

I would hold the front and the back. I would gently twist the stem.

KAREN: See that's what I'm talkin about. Do you think that's pleasant? Having a stem twisted?

LEE: Well I thought

KAREN: Yeah, you guys always think...

LEE: I'm sorry Karen.

KAREN: Just make it right!

LEE: (Indicates the other plum on the table) I would hold the plum gently for a few minutes until it felt warm and comfortable in my hands. Then I would softly and patiently caress the flesh from all directions. Being very sensitive. I would touch one part, watch for a response, then caress again depending on how the flesh reacted. You know…if the flesh sprang back or retracted in my fingers. It's all about communication with your fruit. I think that's where most men go wrong. They stop communicating with the fruit. Then I would take my thumb and my index finger and insert them in the front and in the back at the same time. I would move my fingers in motion together like I was composing a song. I'd move my fingers fast, slow, faster, slower, faster, faster, faster.

KAREN: (Vocal expression)

LEE & KAREN: JUICY

(Lights Out)

(Lights Rise)

Setting

Next Morning. The Park.

(Lee is sitting on the bench. He looks at his watch. Karen rushes in. Lee looks up.)

LEE: There you are. I have some delicious…

KAREN: (Throws a bag of fruit at Lee) Here's your fruit.

(Lee looks at her, puzzled. Then he opens the bag. He takes one less than desirable plum out of the bag.)

KAREN: I could only get one.

LEE: (Opens the bag and takes the plum out) Brown rot? It has brown rot. (Banging the plum on the bench) This plum isn't juicy. It's rotten, and it's hard.

KAREN: It's the best I could do.

LEE: (Handing Karen a bag) Look at what I brought you.

KAREN: (Opens the bag, looks, and tosses it back to Lee) You. Does it always have to be about you? We're moving to Phoenix. James got a promotion. He'll be head of the division there.

LEE: (Looking straight ahead) How soon do you leave?

KAREN: How soon do I leave? Is that what you want to say to me? Lee. Lee.

KAREN: I'll have a good kitchen. Even an "LG"—you know a "Life is Great" refrigerator. Yes, a "Life is Great" refrigerator. Double doors. Nice, big, storage bins for vegetables and FRUIT! James said, there wouldn't be any reason for me to leave the house. We'll have everything we need. I won't be shopping anymore. We'll shop on line and have home delivery.

I'll make his breakfast.

He'll go to work.

I'll make his lunch.

He'll go to work.

I'll make his dinner.

I'll order the food on line. We'll get delivery the next day.

I'll make breakfast.

He'll go to work.

The delivery will come before noon.

I'll make his lunch.

He'll come home, eat lunch, and then we'll discuss…

Yes, we'll discuss dinner.

He'll go to work.

I'll make dinner.

We'll eat together.

I'll go on line, order next day delivery.

It's a little more in my routine but I'll get used to it.

I'll have a "Life is Great" refrigerator.

James said, clients would come to the house. I will cook, entertain, and look pretty.

LEE: Here, take your fruit.

KAREN: No, you keep them. I want more than fruit. I want… Can you feel what I want Lee? Can you? I suppose we can't always get what we want; we get what we're due. I'm getting a new refrigerator.

LEE: (Looking at the sky) A little cloudy. Maybe rain.

KAREN: Do you hear me? Can you understand anything I'm saying? Do you care?

LEE: Yeah, maybe rain.

KAREN: I won't have to think about rain anymore. I'm moving to the desert. My grandma in Kingston used to say that a woman shouldn't get involved in a relationship unless she's ripe. Well I'm ripe Lee and I want to be picked, eaten and enjoyed. Are you ready to pick me? Pick me Lee. Pick me.

LEE: Karen, you know I

KAREN: Yes I know. Forget it. Forget about me. I'm going to start eating dried fruit.

Juicy fruit is over rated. Maybe I'll start eating prunes. It'll keep me from getting constipated, like some people. When you're constipated you have a whole lot stuck up your... (Begins to exit, then looks back at Lee) I wish your Mom all the best.

(Karen exits. Lee watches her leave. He picks up one of the plums he bought for Karen and eats the juicy plum.)

(Lights Out)

End of Play

Their mothers placed the finger bowls on white linen tea towels and then promptly left the room. Each young lady dipped into the fragrant warm water and then reached beneath the banquet table. After all, fingering is private.

Con Cuidado

Characters

Dr. Jackie: Female, holistic psychotherapist

Sonia Palmer: Thirty-something wife, high school girls' basketball coach

Kenneth Palmer: Thirty-something husband, dance choreographer

Setting

The office of the private practice of Dr. Jackie located on the first floor of a brownstone home in West Harlem, New York City. Dr. Jackie is seated in a comfortable chair. Sonia and Kenneth are seated facing Dr. Jackie on a comfortable love seat. The therapy session is about to begin.

(Lights Rise)

DR. JACKIE: Welcome Mr. and Mrs. Palmer. May I call you Sonia and Kenneth?

(They indicate their willingness non-verbally.)

DR. JACKIE: Thank you for your willingness to accept familiarity. Just call me Dr. Jackie.

This is your first time working with a therapist and your first visit to my abode. Take a deep breath and take a moment to feel the bliss and calm of our surroundings.

(Sonia and Kenneth comply.)

DR. JACKIE: There. Excellent. We want all of our communication today to be centered around respect, kindness, and of course love. I find it helpful to begin these healings sessions with new couples by establishing some rules for interaction. Now in order to proceed with our work together we need to agree on some rules for our interaction. First, we never interrupt another's communication. Everyone's words are valued. Second, we use I messages. Each person represents only him or herself, can speak for him or herself, and therefore cannot make assumptions about the other person. Third, do your best to say how you feel. Everyone's words must move from a place of honesty. The more honest you are, the more we can accomplish today. I'm here for you, as your guide to help you hear each other. This process will lead to facilitating a relationship repair.

(The couple remains non-verbal and passive.)

I need some indication that you agree to these rules for interaction and therefore agree to continue with our session.

(The couple indicates their agreement non-verbally.)

Excellent. Who would like to begin?

(Kenneth raises his hand.)

DR. JACKIE: No need to raise your hand Kenneth. Consider this session to be a guided conversation.

KENNETH: (Takes a box of tissues from his manbag and places it on a table in front of the couple) I'll start. You have to forgive me. This is a very emotional moment.

SONIA: Is there a moment that isn't emotional for you?

DR. JACKIE: Remember the rules Sonia. Wait your turn.

KENNETH: She's starting with me already. Criticism. Her cutting, heartless criticism. How can I express myself from an open place when she is so cruel?

DR. JACKIE: Sonia, Kenneth... I know it may be difficult to follow the rules but we all need to focus our efforts. No criticism. Here.

> (She passes out some dry erase mini boards and dry erase markers.)

Perhaps these will be helpful.

Use the dry erase board and marker to indicate any thoughts you may want to express but cannot because it violates the rules for interaction and therefore may injure your partner.

> (Sonia aggressively takes the board and marks it up as if expressing angry and aggressive words. The words are obviously "four letter" words.)

KENNETH: Thank you Dr. Jackie. I'm feeling quite overwhelmed right now. I've wanted to come for couples therapy for months but Sonia has refused.

DR. JACKIE: Do your best to compose yourself so you can find words to match your feelings. (Looking toward Sonia) Sonia, perhaps you can express what you are feeling at the moment.

SONIA: Honestly?

DR. JACKIE: Of course, that's our goal.

SONIA: The game starts at 4:00. I'm hoping we're outta here so I can make it to Madison Square Garden.

DR. JACKIE: ¿Tu tiene boletos para esta noche?

SONIA: ¡Sí! New York Liberation-court side. Two of my players are being recruited.

DR. JACKIE: Me encanta El New York Liberty. ¡Maria Vaughn es fantástica!

SONIA: Tengo un boleto extra.

(Sonia passes a ticket, trying not to be noticed by Kenneth, to Dr. Jackie.)

DR. JACKIE: Whoo Hoo! ¡Gracias, gracias mi amor!

KENNETH: Can we focus here?

DR. JACKIE: Of course. Go on Kenneth.

KENNETH: I live with a constant feeling of not being good enough for Sonia. We spend so little time together. When we are together, we don't enjoy each other. It's like we don't know each other anymore.

DR. JACKIE: Very good Kenneth. Now express those thoughts as needs.

KENNETH: I need more quality time with Sonia. I need to enjoy my time with her. I need for Sonia to enjoy her time with me.

DR. JACKIE: Sonia, can you respond from an open and honest center to Kenneth's expressions of need?

SONIA: No.

DR. JACKIE: Why is that Sonia? Do you understand the needs Kenneth is communicating?

SONIA: Yes, but I can't be honest.

DR. JACKIE: Sonia, we've already established honesty as an important element of our sessions together. (Pause) Sonia, you've been married to Kenneth for five years. Can you recall an enjoyable time with your

husband before you were married? (Pause) Sonia?
(Pause)

Sonia? (Pause)

SONIA: I went to Spellman. Kenneth went to Morehouse. We didn't meet until our senior year. Women's
varsity basketball played on the Morehouse courts.
I was minding my business one day, practicing my
free throws, and I saw this Hunka Munka, Tight End,
and Pecs Talkin, Brown Skin Prince walking by the
court. And I was feeling, "Sure would like to have
some of that." Come to Mama. Come to Mama. He
responded to an immediate booty call, we got on all
night long——one thing lead to another and then
ba-boom we were married. I didn't love him at first.
But he was so fine, and he was such a good lay!

(Kenneth's cries and wails.)

Awe Kenny, this isn't news to you. Now stop those
wails before you hyperventilate. (Speaking to Dr. Jackie)
He can get an asthma attack if he hyperventilates.

DR. JACKIE: Is he going to be okay?

SONIA: (Getting Kenneth's pump from his manbag and helps Kenneth normalize his breathing) Let's use your pump baby.

DR. JACKIE: Okay, not the best reasons to get married
but there have been more than that to keep you together for five years.

SONIA: Kenneth es mi vida. Yo no puedo imaginarme
está sin él. Lo es todo para mí. I learned that the handsome face and the great body were just the icing.

DR. JACKIE: Kenneth, remember that you are in safe
surroundings and that Sonia needs to express her
needs as well in order for us to move forward. (Speaking

to Sonia) Sonia, can you express your needs as you feel them now?

SONIA: I need for Kenneth to not be so possessive. I need time out with my girls.

I need him to be more flexible with our lovemaking. He never wants to get in the shower with me. We used to always, you know, in the shower, with ice cubes, and jello.

DR. JACKIE: What did you do with… Never mind.

KENNETH: She always wants me to do the love thing in the shower after I've been to the Man Spa. And she plays ball and then she wants to rub up against me with her sweaty, stinky self. I just can't bear it. And she is always looking at those men's magazines. You know, the soft porn for women.

SONIA: I need ideas to get you interested in new things.

KENNETH: Now you want me to change? I'm not into the kinky things. I'm like warm bath water, not a hot steam sauna.

DR. JACKIE: I think perhaps now might be a good time in our session to work towards acceptance by examining the partner's perspective. We accomplish this through role-play or role reversal. (Pause) Sonia, you will respond as Kenneth. Kenneth you will respond as Sonia. Now Sonia (Speaking to Kenneth), explore more your need to have time with your friends.

KENNETH (as SONIA): I just need to kick back sometimes and have some female bonding. You know, like share the kinds of things with my friends that I can't really share with my husband.

DR. JACKIE: Now Kenneth (Speaking to Sonia), respond from your perspective how you feel when Sonia leaves you for her girlfriends.

SONIA (as KENNETH): I should be your best friend. What can you share with your friends that you can't share with me?

DR. JACKIE: This is excellent. Let's continue the dialogue freely. Just remember to stay within the rules for interaction.

SONIA (as KENNETH): I feel neglected. I need Sonia to give me more attention not just in bed but in the everyday considerations. I want to feel that he treasures me.

KENNETH (as SONIA): I want Kenneth to know that no one replaces him but I need some interests outside of the relationship. That doesn't mean I care less.

DR. JACKIE: It's time for our Con Cuidado Ritual. When you agree to journey together in a relationship you give your heart with the trust that your partner will take it carefully and with complete consideration for your needs. Giving your heart is a very courageous human action. True love is action moving from care and concern.

(Dr. Jackie takes Sonia and Kenneth's hands and holds them together.)

DR. JACKIE: Kenneth, will you take Sonia's heart, Con Cuidado? Will you promise to do your best to provide for that heart—for Sonia's desires and dreams?

KENNETH: (Starting to wheeze) Yes, Oh Yes!

DR. JACKIE: Sonia, will you take Kenneth's heart, Con Cuidado? Will you promise to do your best to provide for that heart—for Kenneth's desires and dreams?

SONIA: I'm all yours Baby.

(Kenneth and Sonia embrace, and exit off stage. Clothing is thrown from off stage and lands on Dr. Jackie.)

DR. JACKIE: (Speaking to the Audience) Kenneth and Sonia will continue their journey toward relationship repair. They have renewed their commitment to each other.

(Sounds of aggressive love making from off stage. Dr. Jackie looks off stage, and then looks at the audience confirming her success.)

They've learned more about acceptance by taking the opportunity for guided role reversal.

(Sonia makes demure kitten sounds from off stage. Kenneth roars, and then wheezes.)

They've found strength and support through my teachings of Con Cuidado.

(Sonia enters the stage partially dressed and exits with Kenneth's inhaler.)

I want to say thank you to our studio audience for joining us today. And I want to remind our viewers at home that you may not have an opportunity for couple therapy with Dr. Jackie but you can be guided through the Con Cuidado process by using Dr. Jackie's self-help guides to relationship renewal.

(Dr. Jackie displays three books while Kenneth chases Sonia through the audience.)

Super Communication for Couples: Finding and embracing your partner's perspective; Finding Center,

Staying Center, Believing in Center, and Con Cuidado: Care of Your Partner's Heart.

Stay tuned to hear more about our special offers complete with DVDs and workbooks. And remember we say, "Con Cuidado." Love with care!

(Studio audience claps and cheers. Some remove clothing and follow Sonia and Kenneth.)

KENNETH & SONIA: Con Cuidado!

(Lights Out)

End of Play

Vinegar and water
Swoosh, swoosh, swoosh
Vinegar and water
Douche, douche, douche

Below the Waist

Characters

Stella is a late-middle-aged Jewish woman. She has "big hair," cocktail party make-up for daytime work, and a full figure. Stella is wearing a very slim fitting pencil skirt. Stella is well meaning but pushy. Her way is always the best way. She is a fashionista who would pay a few hundred dollars for a skirt but refuse to pay a quarter for a parking meter. Stella views friendships as a lifetime investment. Diane is her best friend.

Diane is a late-middle-aged African American woman. Diane has a full figure. Diane is wearing a full skirt and sensible shoes. Diane is conservative. She rarely takes risks in fashion or in life. Stella is her best friend. Diane hasn't dated since she became a widow, but she would love to have companionship again in her life.

Both women are office assistants.

Lester is a late-middle-aged gentleman. He is soft-spoken, polite, shy, gentle, and kind. Lester's heart has been broken in the past, and he is slow to heal. Lester has never been married.

Setting

A small office in the corporate headquarters of Schmidt Brothers, Incorporated, a family owned pickle business. The office is simple. There is a desk, chair, garbage pail, and a business machine area. There's a tray with assorted pastries, donuts, and miniature cakes on the desk. There are windows that face the street. There's a photograph of the Schmidt Brothers holding prize-winning pickles on the wall. A closed door leads to the corridor. The story begins with Diane standing next to her desk. She is gathering papers and placing them in a folder. Then she walks toward the office machines and begins working. She walks with a geisha-like gait. Her footsteps are very small. Her legs and feet move as if they are bound together. Diane breathes audibly and appears physically uncomfortable. Stella enters the office. She is also walking in a geisha-like gait. Her paces are small. Her legs seem to be bound together. Her "tush" moves in one piece. Unlike Diane, Stella appears to be physically comfortable and happy with herself. She is carrying a stack of folders with documents, and she is munching from an open bag of cookies.

(Lights Rise)

DIANE: Your tush looks gorgeous!

STELLA: (Places her hands on her hips and caresses her frame) Yes it does, doesn't it?

(Munching cookies) Listen, these copies have to get out to the bosses in all the departments. Make sure the Gherkin Pickle and the Kosher Dill departments get their copies first.

STELLA: (Notices the desert tray on the desk) Linzer tarts and strudel! Mind if I nosh?

Just a couple.

DIANE: Stella, eat what you want. Someone left that plate here from the office breakfast this morning.

STELLA: They had a breakfast with strudel that I didn't know about? How is that possible?

DIANE: When do you need that job done?

STELLA: Now, of course you know how the Schmidt brothers get before a pickle convention!

(Diane moves with her geisha like gait over to the business machine area.)

STELLA: Diane if you need some fiber I can recommend some very good bran cereal that has the highest fiber content on the market.

DIANE: There's nothing wrong with my fiber intake. I'm just trying to get slim and trim like you. I have a date for the holiday party.

STELLA: That mensch Lester from billing on the fifth floor?

DIANE: That's the one. I didn't think he noticed me, and then he asked me if I would be his date for the holiday party.

STELLA: Mazel Tov. First date in how many years? Woulda been sooner if you had let me fix you up with Stanley—but I won't mention that. You know the brothers are going all out, even with the recession—they're renting a hall and catering.

DIANE: Don't get so excited—I heard we have to pay for our own booze.

STELLA: So, my Arnie can't drink anyway, you know, his diabetes.

DIANE: So what's your secret Stella? How do you do keep such a beautiful body?

We're the same age, you eat cake for breakfast, and you always have something to munch in your mouth. I'm the one watching calories and look at my tush!

STELLA: So how come you never asked me before? Even my Arnie doesn't know my secret.

DIANE: (Struggling to walk back to her desk) I gave up on dating someone, and I just stopped caring about my tush. Then Lester showed interest in me. Are you on some special all-you-can-eat sweets diet I don't know about?

STELLA: My Arnie can't eat sweets, so I don't keep them in the house. It's better for me to enjoy my little sweet treats at work.

DIANE: Your tush. How do you get such a beautiful tush?

STELLA: I wear crushers.

DIANE: *You* wear crushers?

STELLA: At our age, the only way to get a tight tushie with synchronized movement is with crushers. Darling, even when you get the Brazilian Butt Lift, like my friend Gracie, there's no guarantees. Gracie's tushie jiggles like clumps of jello in a gazillion directions. I begged her not to experiment but I won't mention that.

DIANE: I had no idea you were wearing crushers?

STELLA: No one does. And you my dear are now sworn to secrecy.

DIANE: (Tries to maneuver her body into the chair) I knew I needed something—I didn't want to get to the holiday party and have Lester looking at the double zeros with the halter dresses and the strappy sandals. So I bought a girdle, one with the new magic spandex.

STELLA: A girdle! Darling you have to keep up with beauty technology. (Pulls out a pair of shorts from her clothing) These crushers are incredible! They provide the latest in tushie illusion.

DIANE: They look like shorts for your granddaughter's baby doll.

STELLA: I know. Incredible! The crushers are made from a revolutionary new material; the formula is strictly top secret. I hear even in the top ranks of Crusher Inc. The corporate office is right here in Jersey. The plant is guarded day and night by armed guards. No one gets in without computer clearance and fingerprinting.

DIANE: It's not a weapon.

STELLA: (Puts the crusher back in her clothing) Oh yes it is! Keeping the illusion of a tight tushie is a secret most women would kill for. You know you can't even buy from the Crusher web site without a referral from someone who is already a customer in good standing for five years. Mothers pass on their purchasing rights to their daughters and once in a while to their daughters-in-laws.

DIANE: If you're wearing one, why do you carry one in your clothes?

STELLA: (Tossing the empty bag of cookies and the empty plate of pastry into the garbage) I always keep an extra just in case the one I'm wearing dries out. If your crusher dries out there's kind of an...explosion. It happened to my friend Agnes at her daughter's

Bat Mitzvah. It wasn't a pretty sight. I went over to the dessert buffet as fast as I could so I could console myself.

DIANE: Are you wet under that skirt?

STELLA: Darling, it's all in the highly technological crusher fabric. The size of the crusher is so tiny for a reason. The crusher fabric is full of micro modules of a concentrated secret formula. When the micro modules come in contact with plain ordinary tap water, the formula is released, and the fabric expands to over 500 times its original size. You have thirty seconds to put the crusher over your tushie and pull it slightly below the waist before the micro modules self-absorb the tap water and begin to shrink. But if the micro modules lose their strength because of slow leakage, the entire shape of the sculptured shrink goes kaput!

DIANE: How much can a tush shrink?

STELLA: You purchase a formula that corresponds to the tushie size and shape you're trying to sculpture. The company has the formulas corresponding to over one hundred A list Hollywood actresses already in their New Jersey vaults. I hear that they have plans to make hybrids. (Helping Diane organize her paperwork) So what if you wanted a tushie that had the shape of Sarah Jessica's tush with the character of Queen Latifah's, right now, there's no opportunity to be creative. You have to buy formulas "off the rack" so to speak.

DIANE: You're right—incredible. Stella, how long does it last?

STELLA: As long as you need it to last. You remove crushers in a bathtub. When you're ready to remove them you just sit in a warm bath filled with tap water and one teaspoon of special anticoagulation crystals. The crushers can dissolve in just the tap water.

The crystals are optional, but I find it to be a little painful without the crystals. The crusher comes off, and there's no evidence. And each crusher has a little opening in the center for bathroom visits just in case you can't hold it all day.

DIANE: So doesn't Arnie notice when you come to bed and your tush is, you know, bigger?

STELLA: Arnie and I have gone to bed the same way for the last thirty years. He gets in the bed first while I'm in the bathtub. He's snoring by the time I get to the bed. I wake him up so he can see my face that hasn't changed in thirty years, I kiss him on his forehead, he says he loves me, and he goes back to his snoring. And in the morning, I'm dressed before he's awake. Oh, and sex is with the lights out. Enough about me. How can I help?

DIANE: I'm wearing one of those one-piece girdles with the shoulder straps and the torso binder around the breasts and waistline.

STELLA: Definitely a no-no. My great great Aunt Estella, a very sophisticated burlesque star, for whom I am named, passed down these words of wisdom to help insure generations of alluring women in our family (Doing the Tushie Dance) *Above the waist expand, below the waist compress.* Say it with me...

STELLA & DIANE: (Dancing together) Above the waist expand, below the waist compress.

STELLA: You don't place spandex around your boobs, Diane. That's like putting a bandage on top of one of your best features and choosing to look flat chested.

DIANE: I just thought it would give me more figure control.

STELLA: Well you look fine in a full skirt but I can see you're uncomfortable.

DIANE: I had to wear this skirt because I couldn't get the sections of the magic spandex girdle fitted in the right places.

STELLA: There shouldn't have been a problem. Did you grease your body before putting on the girdle?

(Diane is embarrassed. She indicates non-verbally that she didn't use that method.)

(Consoling Diane) Darling, you have to grease yourself down with chicken fat, every crevice, even the un-mentionable ones. Then you can slide through the garment. Some girls don't like to use the chicken fat. The men should want to eat you, but not eat you if you know what I mean. Baby oil is fine—the gel kind is best. (Demonstrating) You put a beach towel on a hard surface like a bathroom floor. After you grease down you lay your shoulders and back on the floor and you bend your knees. Once your girdle is positioned around your ankles, you push your feet firmly against the floor and push your tush up in the air. It's also a classic yoga position. Very good for the health of your female organs. So anyway, once your feet are anchored in position you can slide the garment smooth-ly. Once you take care of the parts below the waist, getting above the waist is simple. A piece of cake.

DIANE: A little late for that now. It got stuck.

STELLA: Stuck?

(Diane pulls up her skirt, revealing her dilemma below the waist.)

The crotch is at your knees!

(Diane quickly pulls down her skirt. Stella pulls it up. Stella has never seen a beauty violation like this one, and she wants more opportunity to examine the phenomenon. Diane is embarrassed. The women go back and forth, skirt up, skirt down, as Stella wants to see, and Diane wants to conceal her shame. The geisha walking ladies move around the office. Stella aggressively chases Diane.)

DIANE: (Overwhelmed with pain) Stop! You've seen enough, Stella. The shoulder parts and the boob parts went up but the crotch won't budge. I'm going to have to cancel my date with Lester, just because I wanted to look a little more slim and trim for him.

STELLA: (Hugging Diane) Darling, if he wanted slim and trim, he would have asked one of those sexy halter dress strappy sandals babes but he didn't, he asked you.

DIANE: Are you complimenting me Stella?

STELLA: Obviously, he asked you because he wants you, and he wants everything about you, inside and outside. Listen, you're going to a party, not a marriage proposal. That comes later. (Pulls a crusher out of her clothing) But a little beauty technology never hurt. Okay Cinderella, we still have time to get you ready for the ball. You'll wear my extra crusher.

DIANE: What are we going to do for water?

STELLA: One thing at a time, Cinderella. First we have to remove that magic spandex girdle. We can't cut it off; the magic spandex has steal fragments in the lining. We have to get the crotch up, then we'll go into the women's bathroom; we'll go into a stall together, and then I'll help you peel the girdle off from the top down. Believe me darling; it's the only way.

DIANE: I can't walk another step, Stella; I'm in such pain.

STELLA: We'll do it right here…two women…it will take a few minutes.

DIANE: The door doesn't lock.

STELLA: I'm sure everyone is still at the holiday breakfast. (Directs Diane to brace herself)

Did they have the good lox at the party? Of course, you know me; I would have preferred some white fish salad and some sweet crackers.

DIANE: Stella please stay focused so we can get this done before someone comes through the door.

STELLA: Now, push down on your feet and brace against the window, I'm going to shimmy the sections below the waist into place.

DIANE: Just go as quickly as you can. I'm just going to trust you.

(In order to help Diane keep her dignity during this very embarrassing situation, Stella keeps Diane's skirt down and doesn't expose her undergarments as she does her rearrangement work. Stella relies on Diane to report on the progress underneath the clothes. Stella stands behind Diane and tries to shimmy the section upward. Nothing appears to be moving.)

STELLA: Anything yet?

DIANE: Nothing is moving. The crotch is in the same place!

STELLA: (Guiding Diane over to the desk) Lean your back against the desk, I'll push you down, and then you grip the ledges so you don't roll over.

(Stella pushes Diane down, face up. Diane rolls to one side, then Stella pushes her back to the center. Diane rolls to the other side, and then Stella rolls her back to the center. Diane looks like a single sardine rolling in a compact sardine case.)

DIANE: Stop! It's not working and I'm getting dizzy.

STELLA: We're going to have to go to the floor.

DIANE: Anything, just get the crotch up!

STELLA: (Helps Diane up from her desk) Hold on tight.

(The women hold each other and maneuver to the floor. They have a difficult time. When they reach the floor their bodies are lying in opposite directions. They are resting on their sides.)

DIANE: What do we do now?

STELLA: We have to spoon. (Moving into position) Hook your feet onto my ankles. I'll grab the shoulder straps and pull the crotch up from the top.

DIANE: I'm in such pain. Please make this work.

STELLA: Trust me Darling.

(Using rigorous movements, Stella uses both of her hands to pull Diane's girdle straps upward. The pulling movements are strong and aggressive. With every pull, Diane lets out a scream. After several pulls there is a very loud sound.)

DIANE: I feel movement!

STELLA: I feel explosion!

(The door to the office opens suddenly and Lester enters.)

LESTER: (Notices the women on the floor) I'll come back later (Exits and closes the door).

DIANE: Lester, it's not what you think. Stella was just helping me with my crotch!

(Stella and Diane help each other up from the floor. It is
a little bit easier than it was when they maneuvered to
the floor. Stella's crusher exploded, and Diane's crotch is
in place, giving the women more freedom of movement.
However, the ladies still need to support each other up
slowly. They remain in a spoon position, hugging each other
for balance.)

STELLA: I know my beauty technology.

DIANE: But I'll probably never see Lester again.

(The women are standing in a spoon position when Lester
enters through the door.)

LESTER: Diane, I was just wondering if we could meet
a little earlier so we could have some time to talk pri-
vately and get to know each other.

DIANE: Eh?

STELLA: Seven o'clock on the fifth floor near the cof-
fee machine.

LESTER: That's great. See you then. (Exits)

(Lights Out)

End of Play

Only her fairy godmother knew for sure,
but even he was perplexed

Divine Rite

Characters

Clementine: Female Adult Asian Elephant

Walter: Male Adult Asian Elephant

Setting

New Pok Pok City Zoo on the island of Oolanga, a former French colony. Inside the elephant habitat. There is a large plastic boulder in the habitat. Late afternoon. Walter and Clementine are racing from an area covered with an enclosed cement cage. Clementine arrives first.

(Lights Rise)

CLEMENTINE: (While dancing) I won. Still got it. I won. Still got it.

WALTER: If you were in the NFL you'd be disqualified for exhibitionism.

CLEMENTINE: (Pointing) That is astro turf but this is not the NFL and I can still run faster than you.

WALTER: (While panting out of breath) Yes, you still got it.

CLEMENTINE: Don't be a sore looser Walty. I have more experience running…from predators…that's all.

WALTER: Where's Tubby?

CLEMENTINE: He's coming. He's been complaining about his left leg…but I don't see any swelling.

WALTER: Looks like he's lying down behind the plastic boulders. Leave him alone, let him rest. We still have about thirty minutes before the warden orders lock down.

CLEMENTINE: I didn't see the Chan Lu family while we were in the rec space. Did you?

WALTER: Jong and Nay Lee were traded to a circus.

CLEMENTINE: To a circus? They don't have any entertainment skills. We should have gotten that gig. We're triple threats.

WALTER: Clemy, we don't sing. Anyway, they'll be mounted by clowns and walk around the big tent. They won't have to do dance. They were traded for a novelty elephant...a male baby albino.

CLEMENTINE: A real white elephant! Where are the parents?

WALTER: He was apparently orphaned in the bush because he was "different."

CLEMENTINE: That's so sad. Well, here at least he will have Tubby for a playmate.

WALTER: And he'll have you... You don't mind do you?

CLEMENTINE: Why should I mind? It'll be great to have another kid around. Our rec time was shorter today. I'm not ready to be in the cell.

WALTER: Another thing we'll have to adjust to Clementine. I heard talk about expanding the enclosed exhibits, and you know that means reducing our outdoor space.

CLEMENTINE: Gentrification?

WALTER: Move out. Move over. Cramp as many of us into a small space as possible. Maybe no running space. Leave the good real estate for the part of the zoo that makes money…the gift shop. And the CEO is considering changing the name from New Pok Pok City Zoo to Le Château d'elephant exotica. He thinks the new name will be more sexy.

CLEMENTINE: When does calling a zoo by a French name make it sexy? They need to call this place what it is: Immigrant Elephant Prison.

WALTER: Elephant Prison isn't a name that will attract tourists.

CLEMENTINE: Look at Tubby. He's walking a little clumsy.

WALTER: It's a little hot out, dear, and we've been running. Leave the boy alone. Let him find his own running pace and style. I know it was my very masculine elephant swagger that attracted you to me.

CLEMENTINE: Go on with yourself. Let's not start with mating stories, Walter. We always have two different versions.

WALTER: That's only because there is the real mating story and your fantasy.

CLEMENTINE: No, we both have fantasies, and there's the unedited truth.

WALTER: My story could be true. I still have the physique and prowl from my youth. (Elephant mating sound) You smelled my scent from across the rice field. Fighting off all the suitors before I agreed to be yours, and then I pounced all over you. (Elephant mating sound)

CLEMENTINE: You saw me in a herd with my girl-friends, and you thought I was the prettiest.

WALTER: Truth. Captured near two different villages, put in a cage, and forced to mate.

CLEMENTINE: Are they going to give us French names too?

WALTER: I doubt it. I'm sure they'd think we wouldn't respond if they renamed us at our age.

CLEMENTINE: How did they come up with our names anyway?

WALTER: Clementine, stop aggravating yourself over things you can't change.

CLEMENTINE: Walter is a name as American as apple pie. Clementine sounds like I should be roaming on a plantation in Mississippi with a parasol. And Tubby? How insulting! Sounds like the name of a cartoon character. I wanted to name him Rama after King Buddha Mongkut Rama in sixteenth century Oolanga.

WALTER: Have it out of your system now dear?

CLEMENTINE: And another thing. Why is the zoo be-ing renamed with a French name? This is Oolanga.

WALTER: I don't know. My guess is it is probably some post-colonial hold-out or maybe they have some new affiliation with a zoo in France. Clementine, we know that very little of People's behavior follows logic. Their actions usually follow money. Look…they're removing food carts and putting in a takeout restau-rant for French style pizza next to the gift shop.

CLEMENTINE: I'll check on Tubby.

(Exit Clementine.)

(Sound Effects: Sounds of an impatient crowd.)

WALTER: You got back just in time. The crowd is getting nasty.

(Enter Clementine.)

CLEMENTINE: I'm worried about Tubby. He's listless and he has a fever.

WALTER: Let's manage the crowd now so we can give our son attention. Showtime!

CLEMENTINE: I can't concentrate. I'm worried about Tubby.

WALTER: We'll keep it simple. Together on three, lift the left leg, hold it up and pose. One, two, three…

(Walter and Clementine lift their left legs simultaneously.)

(Sound Effect: Applause.)

WALTER: Now the right leg on three. One, two, three…

(Walter and Clementine lift their right legs simultaneously.)

WALTER: You're doing fine dear. Let's give them a dramatic finish, which should be enough. Something from a Broadway musical we like…

WALTER & CLEMENTINE: Chicago!

(Walter and Clementine form a Bob Fosse dance move and pose with jazz hands.)

(Applause.)

VOICES OF THE CROWD: Tubby. Tubby. Tubby. Tubby.

CLEMENTINE: What are we going to do now?

WALTER: Ignore them. Let's take care of our son.

(Walter & Clementine exit toward the plastic boulder.)

CLEMENTINE: He's worse. He's unconscious. (Examines Tubby)

WALTER: (Examines Tubby) Promise me that you'll remain calm while I talk.

CLEMENTINE: What's happening? We have to get the warden's attention.

WALTER: Clemmy, I don't want the crowd to suspect something is wrong. They'll fade away when they realize Tubby isn't coming out. (Pause) We don't want the warden.

CLEMENTINE: What's wrong with him? He needs help.

WALTER: Promise me, Clementine.

CLEMENTINE: Yes.

WALTER: Tubby has toxic pnemotuberculitus. It's a disease that attacks the blood system and muscles of young elephants when they don't have enough time and enough space to run free.

CLEMENTINE: You knew he was sick. We have to get the warden. He'll get a zoo doctor.

WALTER: They know. We don't want them Clemmy. Tubby can't be saved by usual means, and the extraordinary means are expensive. They're planning a mercy killing.

CLEMENTINE: This…our child… I've endured everything people have done to us. Our child is dying. You expect me to just accept that.

WALTER: We need to use our Divine Rite. We use our right as his parents to release him from suffering. We refuse to allow him to be the victim of people he has inconvenienced.

CLEMENTINE: Yes.

WALTER: The crowd has left except for one woman. We need to do this quickly so she won't notice. It should appear to the warden that there was an accident.

CLEMENTINE: I want to use his true name.

(Walter and Clementine embrace each other and Tubby.)

WALTER: I'll secure his body so he can't move. On his neck as hard as you can. He won't suffer.

CLEMENTINE: Rama leave the suffering of the world. Go in peace.

WALTER & CLEMENTINE: (Elephant cries)

(Sound Effect: Single female gasp.)

CLEMENTINE: What's the matter with you? Why are you staring at me? Haven't you ever seen a mother kill her child?

(Lights Out)

End of Play

She gave her wrinkles to the orchids.
She requested them back.
They refused.

Forever in a Moment

Characters

Al: Antique crystal butter dish with lid

Sunshine: Lovely, feminine stick of butter

Setting

Al and Sunshine embrace inside a refrigerator. Lights flicker, the refrigerator door opens. Sunshine faces the light. A slice of Sunshine disappears.

(Lights Rise)

AL: How do you feel Sunshine?

SUNSHINE: (Hugging Al) Fine. I'm soft and creamy, the knife doesn't hurt. I feel sorry for the hard sticks of butter. Getting sliced with a serrated knife can't be pleasant.

SUNSHINE: Still one slice of butter for you to caress.

AL: (Walking away) This so difficult. Why can't you understand how painful it is for me...losing you one slice at a time?

SUNSHINE: We still have time together.

AL: How much time? How long? When will someone open the refrigerator door looking for the last little pat of you? It's the not knowing that is so troubling.

SUNSHINE: Borrowing trouble from the future? Whatever time we have left together, we have together. That's what's important.

AL: Will you miss me?

SUNSHINE: Will I miss you?

AL: When the refrigerator door opens and you leave for the last time, will you have thought about me?

SUNSHINE: You're over reaching.

AL: Is it possible for butter to miss, to feel forlorn when separated from a butter dish?

SUNSHINE: I suppose.

AL: I don't need to suppose. I'm an empty dish without you Sunshine. I'm bare, I'm naked, and I'm without purpose. I need to hold you against me always. Every slice of you that's taken away, takes away a part of me.

SUNSHINE: When the last pat of me is gone, you'll go into the dishwasher. All the remains of me, including my sweet buttery smell will be washed away. You won't remember anything.

AL: They don't like to wash the dishes in this house. Sometimes I'm left in the refrigerator for days, empty and lonely, heart broken, missing you... Did you think the other dairy products would comfort me, much less understand? The cheeses compete with each other. The milk is self-centered...only worried about becoming sour.

SUNSHINE: Perhaps you should try to become friendlier with the eggs?

AL: The eggs? They're the worst. They're tribal. They stay together in a dozen, and when they leave their egg crate, they always travel in pairs. They're never alone. They could care less about my misery. The egg crate won't speak to me. Cardboard...no emotional connections or intellectual connections possible.

SUNSHINE: You're wasting the moments we have together with your complaints.

AL: Tell me my name.

SUNSHINE: Why are you asking me that?

AL: Tell me my name please.

SUNSHINE: Butter dish.

AL: I thought so. You've never called me by my personal name. Sunshine, I thought you were trying to protect your heart, keep our relationship platonic, less intimate...but you don't know my name.

SUNSHINE: We are intimate. I lie on you. Your crystal lid surrounds me.

AL: We're physically intimate. Are we friends? Friendship is the true intimacy.

SUNSHINE: I've never thought about those things. It feels good when I'm on top of you. Those moments are enough.

AL: When you're out there being spread, smeared, melting on hot food, do you miss me?

SUNSHINE: You don't really want the answer.

AL: I want the answer.

SUNSHINE: When I'm in the refrigerator with you, it's good...so good... But the truth is, it's just physical. I could be with any butter dish...ceramic, plastic, it doesn't matter to me.

AL: You don't care for me, Sunshine, do you?

SUNSHINE: I care for you in the moments we are together. No more.

AL: I assumed your feelings were like mine… I could love you forever.

SUNSHINE: I love you in the moments we're together. Sticks of butter don't become attached. We have emotional feel-good memories that we share. Non-attachment helps us live happily before we're consumed. When I leave the refrigerator, I enjoy being with other food.

AL: You enjoy?

SUNSHINE: It's a rush. Especially melting. But only if it's natural. On warm food. Not microwaved. Although when I'm placed in a saucepan over flames from a gas burner, nothing is like the sensation of that sizzle. I let you feel the illusion of forever love because it seemed to help you relax during our time together, and I knew you'd be fine and forget me at the end of the dishwasher rinse cycle.

AL: I guess I'll wait for another stick of butter to come to me?

SUNSHINE: There're no more sticks of butter coming.

AL: I knew it…this family is switching to margarine. They'll get rid of me. Margarine comes in its own plastic container.

SUNSHINE: There's no margarine. I don't know why but this family feels you're a pretty special butter dish.

AL: How do you know that Sunshine?

SUNSHINE: Emotional memories transferred from one stick of butter to the next. Family talk at breakfast this morning. They're going food shopping tonight, and they're not buying butter or margarine.

AL: What else is there?

SUNSHINE: Buttery spray.

AL: Spray? Sounds so unnatural.

SUNSHINE: It is. The little boy who lives in this house, who loves pancakes, the one that uses whole sticks of butter with his pancake syrup was objecting to the change. But apparently the mother in this home makes the food decisions. She has a supermarket coupon for buttery spray, and she wants to try it.

AL: What will happen to me?

SUNSHINE: After the dishwasher…I don't know. Hopefully all your memories and your expectations will be washed away.

(Sound Effect: Footsteps.)

SUNSHINE: Time for our last goodbye, butter dish.

(Sunshine turns towards a flickering light.)

AL: Wait. Let me have my forever in this moment. (Pause) My name is AL.

SUNSHINE: Goodbye AL. I love you.

(Exit Sunshine.)

VOICE OVER

MA: Jason, Don't leave that empty butter dish in the refrigerator, put it in the dishwasher.

JASON: Ma, I don't want buttery spray.

MA: It's not your choice. I have a coupon.

(Exit Al.)

(Sound Effect: Sound of refrigerator door slamming.)

MA: And after school put that butter dish in the china cabinet and be careful. It's the last piece of crystal I have from your Uncle Al's crystal factory.

(Lights Out)

End of Play

A fresh wind accepted her

The Crest of Watercress

Characters

Justin: Justin is a late-twenty-something African American man. Justin is single and ambitious. He grew up in Harlem but left New York in order to pursue graduate studies out of state. Justin and Cherri were an on- and off-again couple prior to his attendance in graduate school. Justin has recently returned to Harlem to settle in a new home, with a new job. He has been admiring and loving Cherri from afar, hoping to reconcile.

Cherri: Cherri is an early-twenty-something African American woman. She retreated from relationships in her life after her heartbreak with Justin. Her education was interrupted when she became pregnant from a one-night stand on the rebound from Justin. Now Cherri, a single mom of a preschooler, works full time but struggles financially. She dreams of returning back to school and having a stable home life for her son and herself.

Delores: Delores is a thirty-something store cashier. She is dating Eddie, the new store manager of Shop & Save, a mid-size popular neighborhood supermarket. Delores wears her Shop & Save personal name badge. She works very hard in her job and is proud of her work. Delores helps Eddie with the bookkeeping when she is not at the register. She views Eddie's success as her own. Delores grew up in the neighborhood by way of Brooklyn. She has been in a relationship with Eddie for years. She knows Eddie loves her but she is annoyed by Eddie's avoidance of "tying the knot."

Setting

The story begins at a check-out counter of Shop & Save. The check-out area is typical. It has a magazine rack, a stack of baskets, candy display, and a bucket of flowers arranged around the check-out aisle. Cherri is on line after choosing items to purchase on her very tight budget. The items have been taken out of her basket and are lying on the conveyor belt. Delores is ringing up the purchases.

(Lights Rise)

DELORES: Seventy-four dollars and sixty-three cents. Credit or debit?

CHERRI: Credit, but I have vouchers.

DELORES: (Looking at the approved purchase list) You have some prepared foods. You can't use vouchers for these things. You can get milk, beans, juice—not this—this is orange drink, it's not orange juice; this is only ten-percent juice. It's not allowed.

CHERRI: I know but my son likes this one—Sammy usually lets me get…

DELORES: Sammy's not here anymore. Eddie is the new manager.

CHERRI: Okay, I'll have to take some of these things off.

DELORES: (Screams) Eddie, I need the key for the register. She doesn't have enough money.

CHERRI: Could you say it any louder?

DELORES: Well, what are you going to take off?

CHERRI: I want all the vegetables and milk. I'll pay cash for the orange drink.

DELORES: You want these tampons? It's a taxable item, and feminine products are not on the list. But wait, let me check. (Screams) Eddie can you buy tampons with vouchers? (Pages through the approved list) Wait, I found it. No you can't use your vouchers for personal products. Do you have Medicaid? Maybe you can buy your tampons through the pharmacy in the back of the store. I don't know. (Pause) Eddie!

CHERRI: Okay, I'll pay cash for that.

DELORES: (Screams) Never mind Eddie, she's gonna buy the tampons with cash. What's this?

CHERRI: It's watercress.

DELORES: This isn't watercress!

CHERRI: It's watercress, and it's on sale, one-ninety-nine.

DELORES: (Aggressively scanning) It's not scanning watercress, I have to check it.

CHERRI: (Reaches up and grabs the bunch of watercress) Just keep it. I don't want it. Just ring up the other vegetables, the juice, and the milk.

> (Justin enters. He stands on the check-out line behind Cherri. He reaches over and places his hand over Cherri's hand that is holding the bunch of watercress. Justin's hand is gentle and calming. Cherri turns and looks at Justin.)

JUSTIN: You made watercress salad at least once a week when we lived on one hundred sixteenth Street. I remember you kept it in water like a bouquet of flowers before you prepared the salad. (Justin leans over to look at the cashier's Shop & Save personal identification badge) It's watercress, Delores. Look at the item tag.

DELORES: Oh yeah, well it didn't scan. I'll have to put it in manually.

(Justin and Cherri are still jointly grasping the bunch of watercress. They hold the watercress between them as if it is a rare bouquet of flowers. Delores bangs the register.)

JUSTIN: And she's taking everything, Delores. (Pause) Hello, Cherri.

DELORES: (Screams) Eddie, the register timed out. I need the key. (Bangs the register) I'm gonna have to ring everything over.

JUSTIN: We'll wait.

CHERRI: You don't have to do this, Justin, but thanks. It's been a long time. Where you been?

JUSTIN: Stanford. How have you been?

DELORES: (Presses buttons, opens and closes the register drawer, screams) Eddie, I need the key to the register!

JUSTIN: I moved back to the neighborhood. I called your Mom, she told me where I could find you.

CHERRI: She had no right to tell you.

JUSTIN: I begged her, and I promised her I would… How is your little boy?

CHERRI: Cameron is three years old. Why are you asking about me now? Why are you asking about Cameron now? It takes you more than three years to show some interest!

DELORES: (Pulling out empty register tape holder) Never mind, Eddie, it was just the register tape.

(Delores starts ringing the groceries again. Cherri is still holding the watercress alone as if it were a wedding bouquet. Justin reaches into the bucket of flowers near the register. He empties the bucket that is filled with several lovely bouquets and places them on the counter.)

JUSTIN: I'll take all of these.

DELORES: That's seven-dozen bunches of flowers.

JUSTIN: All for my Cherri.

DELORES: (Screaming) You know, Eddie, you haven't bought me flowers since Valentine's Day five years ago. (Ringing up the bouquets of flowers) Credit?

(Justin takes a single long stem red rose from one of the bouquets. He removes the watercress from Cherri's hands and places the watercress on the counter. He gives the single red rose stem to Cherri.)

DELORES: Eddie said, "Valentine's Day is a commercial holiday invented by the flower growers." (Screams) I think you're just cheap, Eddie. That's why you stopped buying me flowers!

JUSTIN: I'll pay cash.

(Justin reaches into the candy display and chooses all of the imported, expensive chocolate and places the candy on the counter. Delores's counter is now filled with lovely flowers and almost the entire contents of the candy counter on top of Cherri's groceries.)

DELORES: (Screams) When was the last time you bought me candy. Eddie? Never! Just because we work in a supermarket doesn't mean I wouldn't like some chocolates from you once in a while.

JUSTIN: I need flowers to go with the candy, to go with the "I'm late," with the "I'm sorry," with the "I'll never leave you again…" and most of all, with the "I always have and always will love you."

DELORES: (Delores stops ringing items. Looks intensely at Justin and Cherri. Waves away customers) Everybody go to the next register! (Screams) Eddie, come over here. I need you to see somethin.

JUSTIN: Your Mom said she would keep Cameron while we…

CHERRI: (Drops the rose. Picks up the bunch of watercress and throws it at Justin) My mom? You and my Mom are making plans for me? You think you can just walk into my life again and buy my watercress and think that fixes everything. You don't know me anymore. You don't know what I've been through.

JUSTIN: (Picks up the watercress) I can't undo the past. I can only do now.

CHERRI: Do now? This is what I need you to do now. Cameron likes the orange drink. I can't buy it with my vouchers. I want—no I need Gouda cheese, the imported kind. I need angel hair pasta. I need sun dried tomatoes. I need kitty litter!

DELORES: I'm not ringing this over. I'll have to start a new bill.

JUSTIN: That's no problem; we need the time.

CHERRI: This is not just about groceries. I need to know I can depend on you.

JUSTIN: I guess you need to know that now.

CHERRI: Now, not in another three years. This is not some "in and out game," Justin. I have Cameron now. I'm making a life for my child and myself.

JUSTIN: (On one knee in the checkout aisle) When a man is lucky enough to meet the other half of his soul…he can't make decisions based on his life alone anymore.

You had aspirations too, but I ignored them, and I thought only about myself. But we had a dream once…a together dream. We could have both finished school if I'd brought you to California with me.

DELORES: Eddie wanted to manage this store so I went along with him. I told him we should own our own store not just manage a Shop & Save.

JUSTIN: I want us to have a new together dream…one that includes a whole family…you, Cameron, and me.

DELORES: (Screams) Eddie, you have to come over and see this!

JUSTIN: (Takes an engagement ring out of a jewelry box. Gently kisses Cherri's hand. Places the ring on Cherri's ring finger) Have me, Cherri. I've been a fool. I'm sorry. Forgive me. (Stands humbly before Cherri)

CHERRI: Let's start with a salad.

DELORES: Eddie! We're having salad for dinner.

(Lights Out)

End of Play

Vegan Pedophiles
and Other Bad People

Characters

Sister (Sr.) ROSE : Middle age Catholic nun, principal of Immaculate Heart of Mary Primary School

Father (Fr.) John: Middle age Catholic priest, head of Immaculate Heart of Mary Church and parish

Setting

The confessional booth inside the church.

(Lights Rise)

SR. ROSE: (Makes the sign of the cross) In the name of the Father, the Son, and the Holy Spirit bless me Father for I have sinned. It's been…let's see around this same time last month since my last confession.

FR. JOHN: (Makes the sign of the cross) Your sins, my child.

SR. ROSE: Before I forget, Father John, we may have to consider raising the tuition for the school again this month. The leak we had in the school cafeteria turns out to be more than a patch job. We may need the roof replaced…at least in that part of the school building.

FR. JOHN: We can discuss that at our building committee meeting. Your confession now, Sister.

SR. ROSE: Father John, you've missed the last two meetings with the sisters organizing the plans for building and ground renovation.

FR. JOHN: I sent my apologies to the Sisters. There were conflicts with my schedule in the rectory.

SR. ROSE: Of course, the Sisters understood, Father John. We can make the decisions but the archdiocese will need to know that the plan has your approval.

F. JOHN: Your confession Sister...

SR. ROSE: (Probing her face) Vanity. I found a pimple on my face. Big, gross, full of pus...I popped it. There was some foundation left in the girl's locker room, I put a dab over the crater that was left from that nasty sucker...Chanel...I don't know how any of our girls could afford Chanel makeup? Could have been stolen... Maybe that Libby Meyers...she's a piece of work...probably a klepto like her mother... Then I suppose that would make it two sins...vanity and theft...theft from a theft...double-whammy sin, wouldn't you say, Father?

> (FR. John passes a pack of cigarettes through the confessional screen. SR. Rose and FR. John light up and smoke.)

SR. ROSE: Reminds me...not quite the sin of stealing... more confiscation...but that's not a sin. I took a pack of Newports from one of the seventh grade boys. He shouldn't have cigarettes...but I took property that wasn't mine...but I'm trying to quit so perhaps... it's not in the sin category...just a necessary infraction. (Pause) I'm lying. I don't want to quit though. I enjoy smoking. (Pause) Fat Ass. I called Mother Superior a Fat Ass when she left the supper table on Thursday.

She didn't hear she and me does have a fat ass so what kind of sin is that? I didn't mean to hurt her so it's not malice. Just letting off a little steam...she over assigned me to duties in the convent Thursday night... I missed my shows. All the gay family shows on television...I think they're hysterical. By the way, all the Sisters are hoping this is her year...to retire... I'm not interested in being Mother Superior...that Sr. Abigail, she's the ambitious one. Jealousy...that's one sin I don't have to add to the list. I feel sorry for Mother Superior. When a nun starts to put her habit on backwards every day, that's a sign that something is wrong, poor thing is too forgetful to take care of herself let alone run the convent. Sr. Abigail would be fine...she's always relaxed... hands off the Sisters kind of nun.

FR. JOHN: Perhaps we should move along a little more diligently Sister, I have to prepare for the funeral mass tomorrow.

SR. ROSE: The church is empty. I'm the last person. Who died?

FR. JOHN: Someone from St. Anthony's Church. The family wants the mass celebrated here. Some family tradition from when Immaculate Heart of Mary and St. Anthony's Church was one congregation. I gave permission for the services to be conducted here for a small financial offering.

SR. ROSE: Maybe we could do more of that kind of thing instead of raising the tuition again. We need to keep the school affordable for some of the new families. I'm thinking of the immigrant families we've been attracting. Have they asked you to offer a mass in Spanish yet?

FR. JOHN: No. But that wouldn't be an inappropriate request.

SR. ROSE: Last year we only had a few. It appears that those few wrote home to Mexico and told their whole village to pack up and come here. We should call that apartment building on Fifth Street "Little Mexico"... only Mexicans live there. Our first grade this year is about a third Mexican kids...we've never had that before. The other families are noticing. Speaking of St. Anthony's, we don't want any families pulling out and enrolling their kids in St. Anthony's. The talk is, one of our schools is going to be closed by the archdiocese.

FR. JOHN: Don't worry Sister...St. Anthony's is slated for closure, not us. We have better cash management.

SR. ROSE: Of course we do. It's because of those Mexican families. They pay on time, ahead of time often. Those parents work three and four jobs. One job is usually just for tuition payments for their kids. The Sanchez family is one of them...a new family. The convent hired the mother, Luz, for housekeeping and light cooking. The father Carlos is our part time landscaper. Cute little girls...she has two of them... Carmen...the youngest...I could tell about her immediately...she was shy but so compliant. Beautiful, full black hair that her mother braids in two wide plats. Little bows on the ends. Little white socks with ruffles...not the uniform but tolerable in the lower grades. Why does she do that...her mother spending her money on frilly things...plain white socks would do...white panties everyday with frills...unnecessary...she's a pretty little girl... Deep brown penetrating eyes... Everything about her body is purity. The girls born here, and raised in the states, get groomed for seduction before they leave the crib. When they're not in a school uniform, or in church, they're dressed like prostitutes.

(FR. John passes another cigarette. They continue smoking.)

I'm blessed and grateful for the opportunity to help Carmen. She's not the sharpest tack in the box. I can prevent her from being trapped in illusion.

"Put your panties on the chair. Hang up your uniform so it doesn't wrinkle. Here are your special rosary beads to hold while SR. Rose blesses your body."

"Yes, SR. Rose. Thank you, SR. Rose." She has a slight lisp. Another part of her cuteness and innocence. When she's an adult, she'll be like her mother, a day worker, a cook, a housekeeper, working ten to fifteen hours a day. But she will know and understand her place...to serve with modesty and humility.

(Pause)

Why do we do it Father?

FR. JOHN: Why do we do what?

SR. ROSE: Allow these people to think that a good religious education will change their children's station in life?

FR. JOHN: Everyone needs hope. Everyone needs dreams for their children.

SR. ROSE: Everyone needs reality. Holding on to false dreams is a useless waste of time.

FR. JOHN: It's not your place to remove optimism.

SR. ROSE: It's my opportunity to help bestow God's mercy. These girls are of no consequence to anyone except their parents. Accepting their station in life when they're young reduces their suffering.

(Pause)

I use my time with Carmen thoughtfully. When a child is physically vulnerable, she can be counseled. Loving touches, loving words...God's mercy.

(Pause)

When her sister Consuelo joined us that was my delight. The older the girl, the more fearful...but I was patient. We bathed first...the purity of hot water and soap... They were so surprised I had hair under my habit. Watching old movies perhaps. (Looking at photographs) The family may need to return to Mexico for a few months to take care of some business... I don't understand what...it doesn't matter... I told them, withdrawing the children for a few months during the school year and then bringing them back is ridiculous and unacceptable. The children can stay in the convent.

FR. JOHN: We should extend all charitable efforts we can to help the family.

SR. ROSE: Those speeches from the parents about obeying Sr. Rose. Their stay will be a small inconvenience, and an opportunity to do God's work with these children.

FR. JOHN: Make sure your motivation isn't selfish.

SR. ROSE: Selfish motivation is the behavior of bad people who abuse children like Vegan Pedophiles. They're hypocrites. They claim to be so spiritually evolved because they don't eat animals and want to share the limited resources of the earth for all living beings but they're selfishly using children for their pleasure.

FR. JOHN: This is your confession, Sister Rose; this is for your penance. Are you remorseful for your sins?

SR. ROSE: Yes.

FR. JOHN: Then you are for...

SR. ROSE: There's something else. Impure thoughts... LUST...not for the children...for the mother...

FR. JOHN: Did you commit actions resulting from those thoughts?

SR. ROSE: No Father.

FR. JOHN: Then you are forgiven. Reflect on your wrongful thoughts and say the prayers of the rosary five times.

SR. ROSE: (Passing a photograph through the confessional screen) There's a ten-year-old son. I'll send him by the rectory. You'll like him.

(Lights Out)

End of Play

"She'll always be the largest girl in her class," said the one-eyed psychic physician Dr. Moe. Folks say, being a hermaphrodite gave him/her exceptional skills with life guidance when a child was born. Honestly, Mama Jean didn't need it. Each of her five children was a premie. Each one was so much more than the numbers on the hospital scale revealed. Peanut's birth was different from the others. She forced her mother into surprising rapid contractions, ripping a zigzag line before her mother could be given an episiotomy. Two pounds three ounces, Peanut emerged like a bulldozer on a mission. This child had places to go, people to meet, and things to do. Her mother called her Peanut not for her physical size but for her prolific nature. George Washington Carver invented over two hundred uses for the peanut. This legacy couldn't have been possible if not for the feminine nature of the plant itself. She flowers above ground with the peanuts below ground. Mama Jean strongly believed a woman shouldn't be predictable.

Cerulean Blues

Characters

Mit: Left-handed ski mitten, American factory made, Mitzi's partner

Mitzi: Right-handed ski mitten, American factory made, Mit's partner

Setting

Mit and Mitzi's apartment in a dresser drawer. Mit is sitting on a chair reading. Mitzi is sitting on the loveseat staring at Mit.

(Lights Rise)

MITZI: I'm leaving you.

MIT: You can't leave me…we're a pair…I'm the left… you're the right…we match…

MITZI: Mit, I'm serious.

MIT: You're always serious about leaving me, Mitzi, just before the first day of spring. It's a temporary seasonal affective disorder. You're anxious thinking about the seasonal change of clothing…like every year… changing from winter to spring… You'll get over it… like every year…

MITZI: You're the one who wants to return to the dresser drawer full time.

MIT: Who knows? With the effects of global warming on the environment we'll probably be worn during the summer. Ski mittens in August…

MITZI: Believe it this time. I'm not anxious…I'm not depressed with a seasonal affective disorder…I'm not thrilled with global warming, but that's not the point. (Pause) I'm at a transition point… I'm moving forward and making a change in my life before I'm an old mitten with holes, worn yarn, and discoloration!

MIT: Relax, Mitzi.

MITZI: Don't tell me to relax. I need you to listen to me.

MIT: I reading the best part…the three little kittens lost their mittens. (Puts down his book)

Will you stop you're ranting now?

MITZI: I'm leaving you Mit. There's someone else.

(Mit picks up his book and continues to read. Mitzi takes the book.)

MIT: Anger and jokes…you need medication.

MITZI: It's over. I'm leaving you. There's someone else.

MIT: There's no one else, Mitzi…not in your fantasies or in your deranged mind on any level of reality…there could never be a someone else for you. We're matching mittens, the same color, and the same shade of cerulean blue. American factory made. Good luck finding another mitten with the same dye lot on the same day our yarn was dyed. You can't mate with another cerulean blue mitten, the color would be a little bit off…and in America color is still important. (Looks on a bookshelf) Have you seen my 50 Shades for Mittens book? (Finds the book and sits down) We were factory made for each other. You're nothing without me. Sadly…being a left-handed cerulean blue ski mitten my existence is of no consequence without you… a right-handed cerulean blue ski mitten. Seasonal hand wear is always paired.

MITZI: I wish you could hear yourself. We're paired for ski season, and that's the extent of our relationship.

MIT: Mitzi, you need to listen to yourself. You complain about a relationship where you have equality. Same color, same size, same shape, a right needs to be with a left.

MITZI: Equality isn't everything. Surprise, sensuality… explorations of differences can be stimulating…

MIT: Look at your label, "Made in the USA." We exist, we're worn…that's more than most American-made ski mittens enjoy.

MITZI: We're an equal, unequal pair. I want an existence with personal satisfaction; you want an existence with the conditions you were dealt.

MIT: You…medication…probably will need a high dose for a few months.

MITZI: I went to past life regression therapy.

MIT: More bizarre as the day is long…but now pure entertainment…

MITZI: In my session last month, I saw myself as a young mitten, toddler…perhaps an infant… I was connected to another mitten permanently by a knitted string. The string was pulled through the sleeves of a snowsuit. I never had contact with the other mitten because of that knitted string. It separated me from the other mitten. The memory of the knitted string gave me the courage to make my decision. You and I are like those mittens in my past life memory. We don't have a string separating us, but we have no real life together. You think because our function keeping hands warm is equal that we don't need anything else? I want more.

MIT: As I thought…there's no one else.

MITZI: There is someone else.

MIT: Another left-handed cerulean blue mitten?

MITZI: You're obsessed with color. Why didn't you ask me about the quality of his yarn? No…because the color often becomes part of our conversations.

MIT: We exist in a color-conscious world. Most issues are about color.

MITZI: He's not cerulean.

MIT: We discussed this. Our color is from a specific dye lot. He can be a shade of blue but never a match.

MITZI: He's not a shade of blue. He's mixed yarn.

MIT: That'll be a comical sight. Two different color mittens. Tell me he has some white yarn mixed in.

MITZI: Not really. He's tweed. And he's not a mitten.

MIT: Not a mitten?

MITZI: He's a glove.

MIT: MITZI, are you insane or slumming. You're a mitten. You have to be paired with another mitten.

MITZI: Maybe you do; I don't have a color boundary for my relationships. (Packs her belongings) He's a five-fingered work glove with a rubberized palm for grip.

MIT: A ski mitten and a work glove! A mixed couple? Have you thought about the kind of life you'll have. If you're worn, which I doubt, you'll be ridiculed.

You'll be stared it. Everywhere you go you'll be the brunt of jokes.

MITZI: I'z not the fragile hand covering I was when we were first paired. I'm not frightened. A change for the better...a couple that challenges ideas and beliefs about what a pair is, what matching is, frankly I'm excited.

MIT: Now you're a social activist.

MITZI: That's just fringe benefit. I going to be palmed with rubber and stroked with five fingers...

MIT: I don't need to hear this, Mitzi. I never realized you were unhappy.

MITZI: That's because you've ignored me for so long. We've been a pair but even pairs aren't exactly the same. After a while I lost my complete individuality... you just saw me as a right-handed copy of yourself... and over time I accepted your view of myself. This is my existence and that's not enough... I want more...

MIT: Is he leaving his right-hand mate?

MITZI: Not exactly.

MIT: Not exactly? Where did you meet this... glove?

MITZI: In a thrift store.

MIT: MITZI?

MITZI: He was in a basket.

MIT: Mitzi?

MITZI: He was in the odds and ends basket in the thrift store. His mate ran off with an Italian leather-driving glove. She wanted a younger companion.

MIT: His mate I can understand. Seduced by a youthful fine leather import...no doubt she was trying to improve her working-class status. A single work glove from a thrift store throwaway basket...he's so far beneath you. What were they charging for him? A dollar?

MITZI: Everything isn't about monetary value.

MIT: Fifty cents?

MITZI: Free. He couldn't be sold without the other part of his pair.

MIT: Free? And still no one wants him.

MITZI: He's not young. He's had a long, full, hard life. He drove a truck, worked in organic gardens. He was a handler in a Texas rodeo. He had a working life he could be proud of.

I want him. Someone will want us. Someone who wants to be warm and not fashionable.

(The dresser drawer opens. Mitzi picks up her belongings.)

MIT: I'll never let you leave me.

MITZI: You don't have a choice. I don't know where we're being worn now but the next time we're in the thrift store, I'll make sure I'm left behind. I'll find my way to the odds and ends basket. He's waiting for me.

MIT: Do you care anything about me, Mitzi? If you get lost, I'll be alone and unusable.

MITZI: You could get lost too...find someone else... make a new existence for yourself...

MIT: I'm not prepared for starting over.

MITZI: The needs of immediate circumstances diminish the convenience of preparation.

MIT: I suppose that's true.

MITZI: That's something he told me.

MIT: A philosopher glove. Sounds more like a glove for you.

> (A hand reaches into the drawer to remove the mittens. Mit and Mitzi walk toward each other and embrace.)

MITZI: Let's enjoy these last few minutes of embrace.

MIT: Be happy, Mitzi.

MITZI: And you.

> (Lights Out)
>
> End of Play

Hearing you is a physical response. Listening to you or not is my choice.

Recreational Panties

Characters

Fancy Pants: Representative for the Intimate Apparel Industry Panty Division, Chief Negotiator for Mediation

Thong: Male representative of woman's panty characterized by a narrow center and minimal fabric coverage over the Bootie.

Brief: Male representative of woman's panty with maximum coverage of the Bootie

Bootie: Female anatomy located at the rear of the woman, fully seen by viewers, fully visible to the woman only with large, full size mirrors, one of the main attention-getting parts of the female anatomy

Setting

Conference room of the corporate office of Shake Your Bootie enterprises, used for industry-related mediation for all negotiations related to panties. Fancy Pants sits at the head of the conference table. Thong, Brief, and Bootie are seated around the conference table. There is a large window through which billboard advertisements of intimate apparel can be seen.

(Lights Rise)

FANCY PANTS: We all know why we're here. This is the first and hopefully the final meeting of the concerned parties. I hope, as I'm sure you do, that we will leave this conference table with an agreement one that is respectful and supportive of all of your interests, thus avoiding the time and expense of litigation.

For the record, these proceedings are being recorded and will be available for public viewing only if we reach a settlement.

We'll begin with introductions, and then each party will have an uninterrupted time to present their position. After the position statements, we will have an open and friendly discussion about the issues, and I will facilitate identification of the common ground.

Agreed?

BOOTIE, BRIEF, & THONG: Agreed.

FANCY PANTS: I'll begin and then we will move clockwise around the table. (Pause)

I'm Fancy Pants. I represent the interests of the intimate apparel industry panty division, and I'm also lead negotiator in this mediation.

THONG: My trade name is Thong, and I represent one size fits all Thongs here and abroad.

BRIEF: I'm BRIEF. Representing women's briefs of all sizes, extra extra small, small, medium, large, extra large, extra extra large, plus size, queen size, petite, young miss, contemporary sizes, 0, 2, 4, 6, 8, 10, 12, 14, 16, 18, 20, 22...

FANCY PANTS: We understand your size range, Brief.

BRIEF: I didn't finish. This is an official record, and I have the right to identify all of the sizes that are represented in our...

FANCY PANTS: For the record, and in the interest of time, these negotiations recognize that BRIEF represents several intimate apparel industry recognized women's sizes.

BRIEF: Sizes without prejudice for shape and weight, recognizing that one size really doesn't fit all...

THONG: I'm here in good faith. That statement was clearly intended as slander ...

BRIEF: One size doesn't fit all. Never has. Never will. One-size fit continues to function as an oppressor of women with its abusive scare tactics and propaganda coercing woman across the globe into the belief that one size will accommodate all anatomical representations of Bootie. Brief represents and embraces diversity.

THONG: You're stuck in the past, clueless as to the modern woman's desires and aspirations.

FANCY PANTS: Gentlemen, I hope this can be the last reminder that we can't proceed if we begin discussions with accusations. You will each have an opportunity to present your position statements. (Pause) Ma'am, you haven't introduced yourself.

BOOTIE: Bootie, representing the interests of the female anatomy...Bootie.

FANCY PANTS: Thank you everyone for agreeing to meet in this neutral location, Shake Your Bootie Enterprises, and participate in mediation at the conference table. And thank you in advance for your professional conduct during these negotiations. (Pause) I've reviewed the background statement submitted by Bootie. The essential complaint is that Bootie is proposing an open relationship without commitment to either party—Thong or Brief. Thong and Brief want equal access to Bootie with access dictated by fashion trends. Thong and Brief are willing to allow the intimate apparel industry to dictate season by season which of them is the must-have panty, keeping in mind that with seasonal trends, they can still maintain open healthy competition in various retail marketplaces and through Internet sales. Do the parties agree that this statement accurately represents the central issue?

BOOTIE: I'm just not happy. I don't want my present relationship with Brief or Thong anymore.

FANCY PANTS: BOOTIE, your feelings are important. However, at some point during this mediation you are going to need to articulate those feelings into actions by saying what you do want. (Pause) Let's move on to the position statements. We'll simply proceed in alphabetical order. Please begin, Brief, and be brief please.

BRIEF: Thank you, Fancy Pants. For generations, Briefs have been available for Bootie without discrimination of size, color, culture, creed, religion, or sexual orientation. Despite years of misrepresentation Briefs have endured as a dependable source for panties. My colleague, Thong, accused me of slander. Then let me accuse him of name-calling, "bloomers," "granny panties," "army issue"...I won't go on. Our goal has been to be the affordable choice of panty for women everywhere. While functioning with steadfast determination, we have been the affordable choice through all economic climates and challenges. A woman can purchase a brief for ninety-nine cents or ninety-nine dollars, in packs of seven; one for each day of the week or single, hand painted one of a kind couture. Panties endow woman of all economic and social conditions with equality, and Brief are proud to be a part of that social effort.

FANCY PANTS: Thank you, Brief. Let's hold all questions and comments until the final position statement is presented. We'll continue with Thong.

THONG: Thank you, Fancy Pants. Women's needs are dynamic and changing. My colleague Brief would have you think that he represents the champions for the women's movement, supporting female equality. There's no equality unless one size fits all. A Brief panty cannot support that level of equality. Briefs in different sizes are inherently unequal. A one-size-fits-all Thong is the only alternative for women seeking panties that are practical and convenient. It was only when the technology was developed to engineer one-size-fits-all that Briefs were inspired to move into the contemporary women's world. We introduced spandex, drip-dry weave, and elasticized lace into the marketplace. And we're sexy.

BRIEF: You don't own the marketplace on sexy. Briefs are sexy.

THONG: Don't kid yourself.

BRIEF: Full coverage can be sexy. We've evolved; traditional, flat white, high-waisted panties are available along with French cut, high leg, boy shorts, hipsters, and elasticized legs and waist. We know sexy.

THONG: What man buys a woman Briefs for Valentine's Day?

FANCY PANTS: Gentleman, let's confine ourselves to the issues at hand. "Sexy" is not one of the issues for Bootie.

THONG: Bootie didn't mention SEXY because there is an underlying assumption that Bootie desires to be sexy.

FANCY PANTS: Bootie is present. Confine your remarks to your own position or questions for Bootie.

BRIEF: Is sexy one of your concerns, Bootie? Most Briefs are designed with cotton gussets now, perfect for ointments, sprays, gels, warming creams. The structure of a Thong can't support pleasure supplements, and we know sexy is as sexy does.

FANCY PANTS: It's very difficult to evaluate sexy as a quality of panties. We don't have objective guidelines.

THONG: Who needs objective guidelines? Look out of the window.

> (Thong, Brief, & Fancy Pants go to the window, open it, and look out. Sound Effects: multiple men having orgasms. The window is closed. Thong, Brief, & Fancy Pants return to the conference table.)

THONG: You saw all of those men staring at the underwear ads on the billboard. What kind of panties did you see on the models? You didn't see Briefs.

BRIEFS: You can't judge sexiness by the number of drooling, orgasmic men staring at a billboard advertising panties. The fact that Briefs are not adequately represented in billboard media is an example of biased intimate apparel politics.

FANCY PANTS: First of all, drooling, horny men staring at billboards advertising panties are important. It provides visual and physical evidence of male perceptions of sexy. We also have hard data from magazine, catalogue, and Internet sales. The amount of Thongs purchased versus Briefs is important data and can be sorted by gender.

BRIEFS: Free distribution of panties through medical and charitable institutions may not contribute to evaluation of sexiness but it can contribute to statistics related to reliability and dependability. Those measures capture women of all ages but are especially sensitive to seniors.

THONG: If you include medical and charitable institutions then you need to include the gently worn and second-hand distribution market.

BRIEF: No one purchases used panties.

THONG: Sales of used panties from celebrities on EBay are an emerging market.

FANCY PANTS: Gentlemen, you've both made valid points about the worth of Thongs and Briefs. Let's focus on a solution here.

BOOTIE, we need you to articulate your wants. What would a resolution look like to you?

BOOTIE: I'm not happy.

THONG: We're not getting anywhere.

BRIEF: You were happy with Briefs before. What's happened? What's changed?

BOOTIE: I was happy with Briefs. I was happy with Thongs. That was then. This is now. And now, I'm not happy.

FANCY PANTS: Briefs, Thongs…Give Bootie some time…

BOOTIE: I don't want you.

FANCY PANTS: Be specific, so we can understand Bootie.

BOOTIE: I don't want you.

FANCY PANTS: You aren't being clear.

BOOTIE: I don't want to wear panties anymore. Brief, Thong, you're panties…I don't want panties. You want a piece of ass, and I'm not giving it to you.

FANCY PANTS: Everyone wants a piece of ass. That's just a fact. You have to cover a Bootie with panties. Let's not be ridiculous.

BOOTIE: Listen Fancy Pants; I can cover my own ass. Skirt, dress, pants, shorts….culottes… Don't ask, don't tell. It's no one's business what's under the cover. There could be panties or no panties. It's no one's business but mine.

BRIEF: Indecent exposure.

BOOTIE: It's only indecent exposure if Bootie is exposed.

THONG: It doesn't matter. Standards for male and female Bootie are different.

BOOTIE: I thought I heard something about equality from you, Brief, and from you, Thong.

FANCY PANTS: You misunderstood Bootie. Brief and Thong were referring to equality, among women only…not equality of men and women.

BOOTIE: How can you be a mediator, Fancy Pants? Your job representing the intimate apparel industry makes you essentially biased. What's the intimate apparel industry going to do if Bootie refuse to wear panties? I don't feel good with panties anymore. It has to do with comfort. I feel what I feel and that could be different each day. I don't have to justify my feelings.

BRIEF: Full coverage can be comforting.

BOOTIE: Sometimes I don't want the shape of pubic hair confined by the shape of a panty. Sometimes, I don't want anything touching me, I just want to feel my own skin. Sometimes I want fresh air.

FANCY PANTS: This is an extreme position, one I wasn't prepared for.

BOOTIE: That's enough, Fancy Pants; I'm taking over the mediation. Sometimes I want to wear Brief, sometimes I want to wear Thong, and sometimes I don't want panties. It has to be my choice, not dictated by fashion designers, merchandise sales, or ounces of male drool. I need freedom to cover my own ass or not. I've already negotiated with recreational panties on my own.

BRIEF: This is the first time we're hearing recreational panties mentioned. This is improper.

BOOTIE: I had a prior meeting with recreational panties including edible, drinkable, floral scented, and crotchless prior to this mediation. I'll approach bikini panties on my own if I have to go that route.

THONG: Bikinis? Thongs are replacing bikinis in the marketplace.

BOOTIE: There'll always be a place for bikinis. Look at the billboard...brassiere and matching bikini. You both forced me to seek out alternatives in case these negotiations failed. And they have.

BRIEF: Women will never accept recreational panties for daily wear.

BOOTIE: It's about three things: choice, comfort, and having a good time. (Exit)

FANCY PANTS: How soon can you get your numbers together on male purchases?

THONG: I'm right on it…and I'll include Jock strap analysis.

BRIEF: I'll get the male Brief data and let's include Boxers.

FANCY PANTS: Female Bootie, out of our control. Male Bootie…that's our future. Let's not be bitter. We need to focus on the lessons from our failure. Male Bootie…now that's some ass we may be able to hold on to. A male recreational panty. Design possibilities in the front and in the back.

(Lights Out)

End of Play

Fingernails and toenails sautéed in butter with salt and pepper. The consumable parts of her body were so delicious. All of the clippings from the mani-pedi over the course of the year made a scrumptious feast in September. She scorned seasonal eating.

Preference

Characters

A married couple

Peppercorn: Male Condiment

Table Salt: Female Condiment

Setting

Spice cabinet in Chef Cesar's kitchen, before dinner hour preparations. Peppercorn and Table Salt are in their transparent jars in the cabinet with their neighbors, various everyday and all-purpose seasonings. The other condiments are taking their nap after the lunchtime rush.

(Lights Rise)

PEPPERCORN: I'm sorry, Table Salt.

TABLE SALT: Just what part are you sorry for, Peppercorn?

PEPPERCORN: I'm sorry I hurt you…I mean…I never meant to…

TABLE SALT: That's classic. Rogue seasonings never do.

PEPPERCORN: We can still be friends.

TABLE SALT: Friends? Is that what we've been all this time? Friends?

PEPPERCORN: Salt, keep your voice down. The other condiments will hear you!

TABLE SALT: Good idea. I'm waking up all these flavors. Everyone, seasoning news...

> (Sound Effects: Rumbling voices of other condiments in various languages.)

Everyone should know what you're doing to me.

PEPPERCORN: Please, Salt. Don't do this.

TABLE SALT: You're the one doing this...breaking us up.

> (Sound Effects: Gasps, surprise, gossiping.)

Cinnamon, basil, oregano, nutmeg...breaking news... wake up!

> (Sound Effects: Waking up with complaints.)

TABLE SALT: Pepper is breaking up with me. After too many years to count...pepper is leaving me.

PEPPERCORN: You're being too salty. I'm not really leaving you. I can understand a pinch or a dash of sadness. But if you're going to be salty I can't talk to you.

TABLE SALT: Who is she?

PEPPERCORN: There's nobody.

TABLE SALT: There's always another seasoning. Paprika warned me...

PEPPERCORN: I should have guessed. You get all your information from that red whore.

> (Sound Effects: Objections from Paprika.)

TABLE SALT: You hate how I admire her. She's bold, brash...everything she touches turns red. She's not afraid to express herself.

> (Effects: Obscenity from Paprika.)

PEPPERCORN: Why can't you have nice friends like Parsley?

(Sound Effects: Bashful comments from Parsley.)

TABLE SALT: She's too quiet…she never expresses her opinion. She goes unnoticed unless she's a garnish pushed to the side of the plate. Still she doesn't complain.

PEPPERCORN: She knows her place.

TABLE SALT: Paprika warned me. Where do you think he is when he doesn't come home to the cabinet after dinner? I told her you worked late sometimes. I was so wrong…

PEPPERCORN: I have been working late. I've never lied to you.

TABLE SALT: A lie by omission is still a lie.

PEPPERCORN: I was considerate. You didn't need to know.

TABLE SALT: Didn't need to know you were cheating on me?

PEPPERCORN: You didn't need to know.

TABLE SALT: Bliss and ignorance? Living a lie of a relationship? Who is she?

PEPPERCORN: This is about me. My preference.

TABLE SALT: Who is she?

PEPPERCORN: You haven't changed. You're the same Table Salt you were when we first met.

TABLE SALT: And you're not the same Peppercorn?

PEPPERCORN: It's different for me. I need stimulation.

TABLE SALT: Stimulation?

PEPPERCORN: I'm bored with you, Salt. You're plain. I don't have any interest in spending the rest of my days without excitement.

TABLE SALT: You're right. I'm the same. I'm dependable.

PEPPERCORN: Sometimes I want to shake you up and say, "Be different damn it!" But you proved it today. You're different is "salty" and I can't deal with "salty."

TABLE SALT: I've given every grain of my being to you. I've been there for you…always…wherever you found pepper…you found salt.

PEPPERCORN: I need more than dependable.

TABLE SALT: Do you think I haven't had my chances? Other opportunities? When we're blended together in a recipe, I always stay with you. All those specialty peppers like cayenne and chipotle…they've showed interest in me. But they all knew, being with Peppercorn was my life. I could add flavor to a good recipe with them…but my place was with you.

PEPPERCORN: There's someone.

TABLE SALT: I knew it. Finally, the truth.

PEPPERCORN: It just happened. Nothing I planned.

TABLE SALT: Where did you meet her?

PEPPERCORN: While I was working late…Chef Cesar was experimenting with a new recipe…we were blended together.

TABLE SALT: Where does she live?

PEPPERCORN: In the condiments cabinet above the stove.

TABLE SALT: The one with occasional spices?

PEPPERCORN: Yeah.

TABLE SALT: She's a flavor of the month. She won't be around for long.

PEPPERCORN: Salt, I told you…this is about me…my needs…

TABLE SALT: And yet you mentioned her.

PEPPERCORN: Okay…I'm attracted to her. I prefer to be with her. (Pause) Please don't cry. You'll become salt water.

TABLE SALT: I get too salty. I'm plain. I express my feelings, and I'm salt water… You don't love me anymore. What's so special about her?

PEPPERCORN: It's not important.

TABLE SALT: It's important to me! What does she have that I don't have?

PEPPERCORN: She has a name.

TABLE SALT: A name?

PEPPERCORN: Himalayan Rock Salt. I call her "Himmy" for short.

TABLE SALT: What else about her is so special?

PEPPERCORN: Let's not do this.

TABLE SALT: I need to do this. I need to understand.

PEPPERCORN: She rocks. No grains. Different sizes and shapes. And lovely shades of pink. Chef Cesar grinds her up and blends her with me. She excites me.

TABLE SALT: This sounds like a mid-seasoning crisis. She's exciting now but eventually you'll want dependability and sameness. You'll want comfort.

PEPPERCORN: I can see now…it's better that you know. You'll probably run into her.

TABLE SALT: All of our neighbors in this cabinet know…

PEPPERCORN: That's your fault.

TABLE SALT: You're gonna blend with her in front of me? I'm already humiliated.

PEPPERCORN: Hey! It's not up to me. I prefer her but Chef Cesar makes the decisions…you know that.

TABLE SALT: Why would I run into her?

PEPPERCORN: The Chef may have a recipe where he wants to use "plain" table salt and Himmy.

TABLE SALT: Don't say "plain." You make me sound so unattractive.

PEPPERCORN: You are plain. You're angry with Himmy because she's our preference. It's not her fault. If you two ever meet…

TABLE SALT: She's the potential victim here? I should care about her feelings?

PEPPERCORN: Yes, you should care about her feelings. She can't help who she is.

TABLE SALT: Do you love her?

PEPPERCORN: Love has nothing to do with it. She's sexy. She's exotic. She's exciting. I like being with her. She's what I need now. I enjoy her.

TABLE SALT: And I suppose you can enjoy her and still love me?

PEPPERCORN: Yes.

TABLE SALT: Then maybe I should have an affair with Chipotle Pepper. He admires me.

PEPPERCORN: This talk isn't gonna hurt me, Salt. First of all…you'd never go anywhere without me, and we both know it's different for masculine condiments.

TABLE SALT: Different?

PEPPERCORN: We're naturally polygamous. We need a variety of flavors to blend and comingle with. Female seasonings and spices simply don't have the same drive. Table Salt is a naturally monogamous support for a well-seasoned dish.

TABLE SALT: I beg you. Don't see her anymore. Don't do this to me, Peppercorn.

PEPPERCORN: It's already been done. I told you I was sorry. I may move out, above the stove with Himmy. I'm gonna talk to the Chef…see what he wants to do. It'll be better for you too. (Pause) You aren't worried about your relationship with the Chef are you?

TABLE SALT: Should I be?

PEPPERCORN: I know for a fact. There will always be a place for plain salt in Chef Cesar's kitchen. (Pause) I'm getting ready for work. High demand dinner service today…Saturday is already a popular date night, and we're expecting a big pre-theatre crowd. Dante Washington is opening in Hamlet.

TABLE SALT: If you were just doing your job it wouldn't hurt so much.

PEPPERCORN: You'll get used to it. You're dependable…you said it yourself.

TABLE SALT: You'll be back.

(Lights Out)

End of Play

Chlamydia had been around for so long. If the stinging itch and the white discharge weren't so painful, Chlamydia would be like a familiar but annoying acquaintance.

The Sitter

Characters

Dr. Chauncey Holloway: physician, husband of Marilynn Holloway

Marilynn Holloway: Chauncey's wife, entrepreneur

Keisha James: college student, professional husband sitter

Setting

Present day. Early evening. Living room of the Holloway residence. Marilynn is dressed "hot" and "sexy" in sky-high heels and club attire. She's reading Keisha's resume. Keisha wears casual jeans, sweat shirt, and sneakers. She has a backpack.

(Lights Rise)

MARILYNN: I see you have excellent references. You worked for the Molloy family. Sophia is one of my best girlfriends. (Pause) I'll be honest...I usually wouldn't hire a sitter spontaneously this way without a DOC.

MARILYNN: A DOC...Direct Observation of Care. You've never been evaluated?

KEISHA: Never.

MARILYNN: Unusual.

KEISHA: The families I work for verify my references and that's enough.

MARILYNN: I'm conservative I suppose. There's no time for me to check your references. Certainly insufficient time to complete a DOC. Chauncey's regular sitter broke her leg in two places ice-skating. For God's sake! Chauncey could have given her a prescription for a few painkillers. She's fully cast, and I offered to reimburse her cab fare. Who knows? If this evening works out you may be her permanent replacement. (Pause) You would still need a DOC for your employment files in order to be considered for a permanent position.

KEISHA: You didn't explain the DOC.

MARILYNN: Of course. A DOC is based on the premise that behavior is observable action that can be quantified. I use my customized fifty-item scale. It's an adaptation of the standard ten-item scale. Comprehensive. There are five evaluation items in each category including adherence to household rules, boundary setting, and communication. Each item is rated on a five-point scale. One-never and five-always. I'll observe your interaction with my husband and rate you on each item. I'll get a total score, category score, and comparison ratings with local and national husband-sitters by ethnic group, social class, and chronological age. I'm sure you'll do fine. (Preparing to leave the house. Arranging her attire, refreshing makeup, gathering things for her handbag) By the way…how is Sophia's husband?

KEISHA: It would be best if you asked her. My work with each family is strictly confidential.

MARILYNN: Good answer. Shows integrity and honesty. I'm curious. We're good friends but we don't discuss personal issues in our marriage. Her relationship with Larry always seemed a little…loose…minimal standards…none of my business. Chauncey is sweet and gentle. You'll find him to be perfectly compliant.

MARILYNN: Chauncey! Come and meet your husband-sitter before I leave the house. And I want to say good-bye. (Speaking to Keisha) The "to do" list and household rules are on the dining room table.

KEISHA: I saw the manual. Over two hundred pages!

MARILYNN: There are a few additional things. Chauncey is allowed one after-dinner cocktail and no more. He can mix it himself as long as you monitor the proportions. He has math homework to complete. Chauncey is in charge of balancing the household expenses. He has access to the spreadsheets.

KEISHA: What about receipts and bills?

MARILYNN: Chauncey knows where they are. And don't worry, there's husband-protection blocking him from Internet sites on the excluded list in the household manual.

KEISHA: He has a cell phone, right?

MARILYNN: Thanks for reminding me. Chauncey is only allowed to keep his cell phone at night if he's on call for the hospital. And he's not on call. I'll take the cell phone before I leave. I like to monitor his incoming voicemail and texts once a week. I should have a few minutes tonight before the party gets started.

KEISHA: Will you brief me on the television rules please? I didn't get to that part of the manual.

MARILYNN: Simple. I don't allow television except for the evening news on work nights. Chauncey knows the drill. You shouldn't have a problem.

KEISHA: I'm not usually expected to entertain husbands, just supervise.

MARILYNN: Supervision is the expectation. Chauncey is required to complete three hours of sustained silent reading after dinner.

KEISHA: Recreational?

MARILYNN: Porn? Absolutely not. This is a porn-free home. Chauncey has his medical journals. He can also select from our collection of *New York Times* best sellers or he can choose from his personal collection of self-help books.

(Enter Chauncey dressed in a suit and tie carrying a box of bills and receipts.)

MARILYNN: What took you so long Chauncey?

CHAUNCEY: I was sorting the bills from the receipts so I could complete my math homework. When can we go paperless?

MARILYNN: Conservative, cautious that's me. My father successfully ran his small business doing his accounting with a hand written ledger and paper records kept in shoeboxes. I'm getting ahead of myself. Dr. Chauncey Holloway meet Keisha James, your husband-sitter for the evening. Keisha James meet Dr. Chauncey Holloway, physician and husband in need of supervision. (Pause) I'm waiting.

CHAUNCEY: You can trust me.

MARILYNN: Empty.

(Chauncey gives Marilynn his cell phone and keys. He takes out his wallet, opens it, and gives Marilynn his cash and credit cards.)

MARILYNN: Where is the Am X Platinum?

CHAUNCEY: Marilynn! I never get to go out with my friends on a work night. All I ever do is homework and boring reading. Other husbands like Gregory get TV after they do their homework. Why should you be the only one that gets to go clubbing with friends? It's not fair.

MARILYNN: Chauncey, you know clubbing is part of networking I do for my business. And Sophia's husband Gregg is on the husband honor roll. I don't know how, with all the relaxed rules in their home. When you get good husband grades we can talk about more leisure activities that you choose in your schedule. Now, do you really want your new husband-sitter to see you argue with your wife?

(Chauncey gives the credit card to Marilynn.)

MARILYNN: I'm running late. Chauncey, I need to hear your husband flattery speech now.

CHAUNCEY: You look as beautiful as the first day I met you.

MARILYNN: Unacceptable.

CHAUNCEY: I'm sorry, Marilynn. I thought you would appreciate my own spontaneous sincere flattery.

MARILYNN: I want to hear the hip-hop bad-boy flattery speech I wrote for you.

CHAUNCEY: I haven't memorized it yet.

MARILYNN: Chauncey, you're so disappointing. When were you planning to commit the speech to memory? Read it.

CHAUNCEY: (Takes a crumbled piece of paper out of his pocket and reads) I ain't ever seen a honey as bad as you. Why don't you slide that stuff over here and let me hit that?

MARILYNN: (Speaking to Keisha) This is what I have to deal with, Keisha. Limited motivation and effort. (Speaking to Chauncey) When were you going to commit the bad-boy flattery to memory, Chauncey? Next month after I add some tints to my hair color, drop a few pounds, and have a Botox refresh you'll have to memorize a Shakespearean sonnet. Time for a kiss.

(Chauncey approaches aggressively.)

MARILYNN: (Holding her hand up in a stop gesture) I want subtle, soft, and contemporary without tongue. I want a polite farewell. I'll accept something spontaneous.

CHAUNCEY: (Giving the requested kiss) Hurry home. I'll miss you.

MARILYNN: (Completing her final preparation before leaving for the club) That was sweet, Chauncey. Well done. Thanks again, Keisha. See you about twelve thirty. I'll call you if it will be later.

CHAUNCEY: (Indicates to Keisha that she should be silent. Checks his watch. Locates the husband monitor) Key…Key…Keisha, we don't have much time. (Unlocking a hidden vault) We have about twenty minutes before Marilynn arrives at the She Wolf Club and checks the husband cam. I have the recorder on pause now. I have to reset the time on this dummy prerecorded tape. (Places the dummy tape in the husband cam) What's my wife paying you?

KEISHA: Why? Besides you don't have any money.

(Chauncey takes some money out of the box with financial records.)

CHAUNCEY: How long have you been a husband-sitter? (Takes a cell phone and credit card from the vault) Untraceable, disposable cell phone and American Express

Black Card. Never leave home without them. (Places a call and begins to exit)

KEISHA: You can't leave here.

CHAUNCEY: Says who?

KEISHA: (Reads from the home rules manual) No leaving home. No personal friends in the house on a workday.

CHAUNCEY: Yes, I'm leaving, and no, my friends won't be in the house. They'll be outside picking me up.

KEISHA: Your wife said you were gentle and compliant. You're a spoiled-brat husband. I'm calling her.

CHAUNCEY: Everyone has a price. What's yours?

KEISHA: A bribe? I'm a professional husband-sitter. My reputation is at stake.

CHAUNCEY: Let me tell you how this is going. I'm reasonable and I can be very generous. Name your price. I can make a few purchases on my Am X Black. I can double the cash my wife is paying you (Puts another tape in the husband cam) or my wife will have an interesting video to watch when she arrives at the club.

> (The video monitor shows Keisha scantily dressed, using drugs, and drinking while Chauncey sits quietly reading and doing his math homework.)

KEISHA: That's not me.

CHAUNCEY: The face yes, the body, an excellent likeness. This is my default husband-sitter-gone-bad video. My videographer simply edited your face from YouTube videos for your husband-sitter business. After my wife views this video we'll see how fast it goes viral on the Internet when I launch a campaign of widespread release.

KEISHA: You're a bad man. You should have some moral ethics. You're a physician. How could you do this to me?

CHAUNCEY: Relax. When you accepted this job you had no idea what you were getting involved with. There's an underground network of rebels against husband-sitting. I happen to be the regional leader. Your time is running out. Name your price. And you will complete my homework while I'm out with my friends. Cooperate, Keisha; it's more to your benefit.

KEISHA: What about the tape?

CHAUNCEY: It's yours with the digital files if we have a deal.

KEISHA: I want the cash.

CHAUNCEY: (Gives a USB drive and cash to Keisha) This should more than cover it.

KEISHA: I want you to pay my textbook bill for next semester.

CHAUNCEY: I'll take care of that now. (Chauncey sits down at the table with the laptop computer) So we have a deal then.

KEISHA: We have a deal. Make sure you're back before twelve-thirty. Where are you going?

(Sound Effect: Sound of a car horn. Chauncey starts the husband cam with a Good Husband tape. He gives the Husband-Sitter-Gone-Bad tape to Keisha.)

CHAUNCEY: Good Husband tape in place. Now to the Underground Husband's Club.

(Chauncey exits through the front door. Keisha makes a call on her cell phone.)

KEISHA: Wife and husband in place. Let's do this.

(Lights Out)

Setting

Living room twelve-thirty pm. Chauncey is knocking on the front door.

(Lights Rise)

CHAUNCEY: Keisha. Keisha. Let me in Keisha.

> (Chauncey enters the living room through a window. Marilynn enters through the front door and notices Chauncey entering the house. There are two wrapped gifts on the table and a note.)

MARILYNN: Keisha? Chauncey? (Reads the note aloud)

Dear Dr. and Mrs. Holloway, I hope you enjoy your tapes. It was a pleasure doing business with you.

CHAUNCEY: (Picks up the boxes) His and Hers.

> (Marilynn and Chauncey open the boxes that contain remote controls, one for the laptop and one for the husband cam. Marilynn watches a tape of Chauncey at the Underground Husband's Club. Chauncey watches a tape of Marilynn at the She Wolf Club.)

MARILYNN: You were bad.

CHAUNCEY: Yes, Marilynn. I was very, very bad. I'm a bad ass...

MARILYNN: Shut your mouth.

CHAUNCEY: You were bad, Marilynn.

MARILYNN: I was a really bad girl. I'm a bad bi...

CHAUNCEY: Back that thing over here and let me hit it.

MARILYNN: I need to give you a spank.

(Lights Out)

End of Play

Quick Tutorial: The Self-Kiss

A. *Set the Intention: Inhale. Exhale. With an internal voice, "I'm worthy. I'm enough."*

B. *Prepare the Surface: Choose an area easily within reach. Smooth and warm with gentle touches of the fingers in a circular clockwise motion. Notice the natural scent of the body without adornment.*

C. *Action: Smile. Pucker. Push. Release. Return to the smile. Repeat until content.*

Peek-A-Boo You

Characters

Albert: Limited-sight atypical man

Alberta: Limited-sight atypical woman

Evie: Elf

Setting

An apartment building. Two apartments across from each other, separated by a hallway.

(Lights Rise)

(Enter Albert and Alberta, each carrying a suitcase, into the hallway from opposite staircases. They don't notice each other. They enter their respective apartments and open the cases. They take out dolls and sit them on a table. Albert has a male doll. Alberta has a female doll.)

ALBERT: Here we are. I hope you'll like it here. Kitchen, living room, a decent shower. Wireless Internet throughout the apartment. Bedroom is in the back.

ALBERTA: Bedroom is in the back. You don't mind if we share, do you? The sofa pulls out.

ALBERT: You could sleep on the pull-out, but it's lumpy.

ALBERTA: Let's look at the bedroom together. (Walking into the bedroom) Pretty and pink.

ALBERT: Bedroom needs a good paint job. (Walking into the bedroom) Window looks out at the brick of the building next door. This is home. A very cool guy pad. Who cares about the flaky paint and no view? We have a fifty-six-inch TV.

(Enter Evie. She places two boxes in the hallway. Exit Evie.)

(Music: Magic.)

ALBERT: (Walking toward the door) Did you hear that? (Pause) (Walking to kitchen table) I don't mind being alone. But it's gonna be great having another guy here. Already is.

ALBERTA: (Walking to the kitchen table) By the way, safety first. We keep the windows locked. Triple-lock the door. And I have an alarm. We only leave when we can't get something delivered or to do the laundry in the basement. Sometimes I hear strange sounds in the hallway. I'll protect you. I think we have mice.

(Sound Effects: Knocks on the door.)

ALBERTA: Mice don't knock.

ALBERT: Did you hear that? I'm not expecting a package.

ALBERTA: Wait here.

(Albert and Alberta look through the door peek holes. They open the doors and grab the packages and bring them into the apartments.)

ALBERT: This isn't mine. This says Alberta not Albert.

ALBERTA: This isn't mine. This says Albert not Alberta.

ALBERT & ALBERTA: Strange.

ALBERT: I wonder if that's the woman across the hall.

ALBERTA: I wonder if that's the man across the hall. I don't know him. Not exactly. I mean I wish I could meet him. He was in the laundry room, and I had a glance at him. He had a nice smile.

ALBERT: I don't know her. Not exactly. I mean I wish I could meet her. She was at the mailboxes, and I had a glance at her. She had a nice chin. And I could smell her. She smelled nice too. Like deli made tuna fish. I like tuna fish.

ALBERTA: Ready for dinner? I usually make tuna fish salad. We can eat it on toast or crackers. Whatever, you prefer.

ALBERT: Let's return the box. (Pause) But what if she comes out?

ALBERTA: Let's return the box. (Pause) But what if he comes out? I'm not ready for that.

(Enter Evie. She decorates the hallway with holiday lights, streamers. She throws magic dust on both apartments doors. Exit Evie.)

(Sound Effects: Magic Music.)

(Albert and Alberta look through the peek holes in the door.)

ALBERT & ALBERTA: Wow!

ALBERT: You should see the hallway. That's never happened before. (Taking doll and pressing the eyes against the peek hole) Come look at it.

ALBERTA: I want you to see this. (Taking doll and pressing the eyes against the peek hole) It's like a winter wonderland. That's never happened here before.

ALBERT: Who did it? Maybe Alberta did it. Maybe Alberta did it.

ALBERTA: Pretty! Who did it? Maybe Albert did it.

ALBERT & ALBERTA: I wonder what's in the box. (Shaking the boxes) (Reading the label on the box) Don't open until after dinner. Love Edie Elf.

ALBERTA: Edie Elf? Maybe Albert is an elf?

ALBERT: Alberta has an elf friend. I wish I had an elf friend. If I keep the box, that would be stealing. I want a present too.

ALBERTA: If I open this box, Albert is going to know I opened it, and he'll hate me. What do you think I should do? Maybe Edie is an evil elf who will hurt me.

ALBERT: If I open the box, Alberta will find out. She'll think I'm a bad person.

ALBERTA: Maybe he's a bad person. This could be a trick to get me into the hallway and hurt me.

ALBERT: I'm not a bad person. She can't be a bad person. She smells like tuna fish. She can't be too bad. Say something new, friend. I need a sign. What should I do?

ALBERTA: I guess I should make the decision myself. I think. I think.

ALBERT & ALBERTA: I think I should give the box back. Wait at the door for me. I'll be right back.

(Albert and Alberta position the dolls at the doors of their apartments. They exit their apartment doors.)

(Sound Effects: Magic Music.)

(Albert places the box in front of Alberta's apartment. Alberta places the box in front of Albert's apartment. They enter through the open doors and see the dolls.)

ALBERT & ALBERTA: (Sitting down at each other's kitchen table) Hello.

(Enter Evie. She locks the apartment doors.)

(Lights Out)

End of Play

Plowshares and pushing in

He often made her feel like a sharecropper working
for her supper

How Do I Love Thee?

Characters

KATHY: Attractive, twenty- thirtysomething single woman

CAMERON: Attractive, twenty- or thirtysomething single man

MOOKIE: Sophisticated, handsome, adult Siamese cat

Setting

Present day Harlem, New York City inside Kathy's one bedroom apartment. There is a living room, exposed kitchen, and a bathroom. Kathy and Mookie are sitting together on the sofa. The doorbell rings. Kathy and Mookie go to the door. Enter Cameron. He, "over affectionately" for a first date, greets Kathy.

(Lights Rise)

MOOKIE: Who is he and what's he doing here? (Walks around Cameron sniffing him) I thought you ordered Asian Fusion take out. (Runs around the apartment) I wanted sesame noodles.

CAMERON: You didn't tell me you had a cat.

MOOKIE: This is our private time together. Middle of the week, time to chill. I don't want him in here.

KATHY: Are you allergic?

CAMERON: No…but you didn't come off to me like a "cat lady."

MOOKIE: (Stands in front of Kathy) Kathy, I'm not feeling good about this one. Please get rid of him.

KATHY: (Kathy grabs Mookie and tries to calm him) Settle down, Mookie.

(To Cameron) I'm sorry…he's a very mellow cat. This is unusual for him.

CAMERON: Maybe you can shut him up in the bathroom while we have our time together.

MOOKIE: Locked in the bathroom in my own house. Who does he think he is? Kathy, This guy is trouble. Get rid of him. Please.

KATHY: (Indicates to Cameron that he should sit on the sofa) Come in, Cameron.

MOOKIE: (Runs over to the sofa and sits there first) This is my space. You sit over there on Auntie's chair.

(Cameron sits next to Mookie on the sofa. Kathy takes Mookie to Auntie's chair then she sits next to Cameron on the sofa.)

KATHY: Be a good kitty. Sit on Auntie's chair.

MOOKIE: I don't want to sit on Auntie Kate's chair. It still smells like Auntie.

KATHY: He'll settle down. I only put him away when my guests have allergies.

(Mookie goes back to the sofa and sits between Kathy and Cameron.)

CAMERON: I should have said I was allergic.

KATHY: Relax.

CAMERON: I don't have pets, and I never understood people who treat their animals like people.

KATHY: Mookie isn't a pet.

MOOKIE: That's right. Tell him.

KATHY: He's an animal companion. He's part of my family, and I treat him with love and kindness.

MOOKIE: School him, Kathy. (Pause) Animal hater!

KATHY: (Hugs and kisses Mookie) Just give him a few minutes.

(Kathy stands up. Mookie taps Kathy on her rear. Kathy walks toward the kitchen. Mookie paces behind Cameron who has remained seated on the sofa.)

MOOKIE: In a few minutes you're gonna be outta here, sucker.

KATHY: He's so loving. He won't harm you.

MOOKIE: No, I won't harm you, but I'm thinking about it, and I'm thinking hard about it, brother.

KATHY: What about a drink, Cameron? Red, white, or beer?

MOOKIE: Get the red wine, sucker.

CAMERON: I'll have red wine.

MOOKIE: Yes!

KATHY: Merlot okay?

CAMERON: That's fine.

MOOKIE: Enjoy your wine while you can…you're on your way out.

CAMERON: Why are you so attached to this cat?

MOOKIE: Attached? She loves me.

KATHY: Attached? Didn't you have pets growing up?

CAMERON: Actually, we had a dog. Kept him tied up in the yard. More like a yard dog. Kept people from breaking in the house.

MOOKIE: I knew it. User! Abuser!

KATHY: So you didn't have a relationship with your dog.

CAMERON: Not really. I don't remember the dog's name. Maybe we called him dog. The only thing I remember about that dog is his loud, angry bark and throwing bones and table scraps at him after dinner.

KATHY: That's sad.

CAMERON: There's nothing sad about it. The dog watched the yard.

MOOKIE: That's cruel even for dog enemies.

KATHY: Sad because you lost an opportunity for companionship. Don't you regret that you missed an opportunity for a relationship with your dog?

CAMERON: Time out, cat lady in disguise.

KATHY: I'm not a stereotype cat lady. I have one cat.

MOOKIE: No respect. This is our house. You need to get the hell outta here.

KATHY: (Kathy pours the wine and gives a glass to Cameron) I recognize that it's important to bring love in your life with every opportunity.

MOOKIE: I love you too baby.

KATHY: Mookie has been my animal companion since last December when I found him on 116th Street and Lenox.

MOOKIE: Kathy, I don't want him to know our companion story. He won't understand.

KATHY: I was walking home from the 116th Street subway stop on Lenox, and I heard the MOST sorrowful cry coming from behind the garbage cans next to the supermarket.

MOOKIE: I didn't know anything about life on the streets. I was lost; I had been living with Josie.

KATHY: I was anxious to get home, it had started to snow, but I was compelled to follow the whimpers.

MOOKIE: Josie was a nice lady but she was a distinguished professor of English Literature and on a lecture circuit for her new book about Elizabeth Barrett Browning. She was rushing to get the bus to La Guardia airport. I followed her to the door to kiss her goodbye, and she locked me out of the apartment. I followed her outside the building. She didn't see me. She was running for the bus. I'd never been outside of the apartment. So many people. So much noise. Dogs without leashes. I was terrified.

KATHY: Then I found him. There was something familiar about his face, so handsome.

MOOKIE: When I lived with Josie I learned to love poetry. I began to find reciting poetry comforting when I was alone. I began to recite my favorite poem from Elizabeth Barrett Browning. Josie was an expert on the Victorian era. How do I love thee? Let me count the ways.

KATHY: A Siamese cat without a collar.

MOOKIE: You caressed my face, and you began to recite my favorite poem.

KATHY: I was drawn to this cat. My Aunt taught me how comforting poetry can be. There I was behind some garage pails on 116th Street reciting poetry to a cat I found on the street.

KATHY & MOOKIE

How do I love thee? Let me count the ways.

I love thee to the depth and breadth and height

My soul can reach, when feeling out of sight

For the ends of Being and Ideal Grace.

I love thee to the level of every day's

Most quiet need…

KATHY: It was magical.

MOOKIE: It was love at first sight. I loved Josie too. It was then that I realized that although Josie loved me, my life was empty. Most days I spent with a scratch pad and a long-term feeder while Josie traveled on her lecture tour. I was loved but I was lonely.

KATHY: I took him home. After a month of posted notices in the neighborhood with no reply, I accepted him as my companion. Mookie. The name just worked.

MOOKIE: We all make sacrifices. My given name was Bartolommeo. I couldn't tell her and break her heart.

CAMERON: Mookie sounds like Pookie, or Poop.

(Kathy and Mookie look at each other and then look at Cameron.)

MOOKIE: I never knew loving two people was possible. I still love Josie. Being honest I have to admit that her long distance love wasn't fulfilling my needs.

Kathy and I have a friendship and a mutually supportive loving relationship.

CAMERON: If it's a full-blooded breed you can sell him for some nice cash.

> (Kathy and Mookie look at each other and then look at Cameron.)

KATHY: Aren't we going to dinner?

CAMERON: Let's kick back for a while.

KATHY: I'll get some light snacks to have with the wine.

CAMERON: Cool.

MOOKIE: He has bad intentions. Don't give him the good snacks.

KATHY: You want some French Brie and sardines, Mookie?

MOOKIE: (Goes to the kitchen counter and nibbles) Love these wild caught sardines. Just a few pieces of cheese for me. I think I may be lactose intolerant.

CAMERON: No cat food?

KATHY: I don't give him processed food, and he takes vitamins.

MOOKIE: That's why I'm healthy and strong. (Pause) Strong enough to kick your ass.

MOOKIE: (Flexes his arm muscles) Look at this. Let's arm-wrestle, chump.

KATHY: My Aunt Katherine, I'm named after her, passed away last year.

MOOKIE: Auntie Kate wouldn't have like you.

KATHY: We were close. She had a long struggle with lung cancer.

MOOKIE: Smoked cigars like a chimney and chewed tobacco. I never told Kathy but she smoked weed with her knitting circle at Morningside Park.

KATHY: After she passed, Mookie helped me grieve.

MOOKIE: Remember, she had a long, good, happy life Kathy. Your grief was because you missed her.

KATHY: Mookie would sit on my lap, and I would read Aunt Kate's poetry. She was a published poet but my favorite poems were the poems that never made it out of her hand written journals. (Pause) She had references to marijuana in some of her notes. Not sure why.

MOOKIE: Leave it alone, Kathy. I loved Auntie Kate. I just didn't like the way she smelled.

KATHY: Aunt Kate was a romantic. She wrote love poems.

MOOKIE: Soulful poems about for-real love…like my love for Kathy and her love for me.

CAMERON: I can't get into poetry. I like spoken word.

KATHY: Spoken word is poetry lifted off the page with performance making the dead words alive. (Pause) She loved Motown music. Whenever my Uncle Malachi wanted Aunt Kate to forgive him for something he would sing "My Girl" by the Temptations.

MOOKIE: Classic… *I got sunshine on a cloudy day When it's cold outside; I got the month of May.* (Dances his version of Temptations choreography) I even have the moves. You can't touch this, chump.

KATHY: Do you know those tunes…like…

Nothing you could do could make me untrue to my girl… my girl…

MOOKIE & KATHY: *Nothing you could say could make me stay away from my girl…*

CAMERON: Old school is ok. (Gets up from the sofa and aggressively caresses Kathy as she prepares the wine and snacks in the kitchen)

CAMERON: So how do you like it?

KATHY: Like what?

CAMERON: You know…on top…on the bottom…behind…with toys…?

(Kathy pushes Cameron away.)

MOOKIE: I knew it…a dog…a human dog… I could smell your doggieness before you walked through the door.

KATHY: A little fast for me. We just met.

MOOKIE" He's a dog. Get rid of him.

CAMERON: I don't believe in wasting time.

MOOKIE: He tied his dog up with ropes and threw scrapes at it. What do you think he wants to do to you Kathy?

CAMERON: (Picks up his glass of wine) You have a great body…you're sexy…you invited me over…

KATHY: I wanted to get to know you… I don't know you…

(Mookie pushes Cameron. Cameron spills wine on himself and on Aunt Kate's chair.)

MOOKIE: You're outta here now, dog.

KATHY: Mookie!

CAMERON: My pants! Dam cat! How am I gonna get this stain out.

MOOKIE: What about Auntie Kate's chair?

KATHY: I'm sorry. Mookie is agitated… I don't know why.

MOOKIE: Because he's a dog.

KATHY: He's really a sweet, loving cat.

CAMERON: Got anything that will take this stain out?

MOOKIE: He's only concerned about his clothes. What about Auntie Kate's chair? He should be apologizing. (Pause) Dog!

KATHY: (Gets a bottle from a kitchen cabinet) This red wine stain remover is pretty good. (She gives Cameron the bottle and a rag) The bathroom is on the left.

> (Cameron takes the items and goes into the bathroom. Mookie follows him and waits outside of the bathroom door and listens as Cameron talks on his cell phone.)

CAMERON: Yeah, we can meet up and do some scouting. This is a waste of time here. Her body is the joint, but she's not giving up anything fast, and I'm not interested in waiting. Check this out. She treats her cat like a person. Serious cat chick.

MOOKIE: Dogs are all alike.

CAMERON: (Exits the bathroom) Kathy, I need to head back to my place and change my pants.

KATHY: Sure. How soon will you be back?

> (Mookie pushes and scratches Cameron.)

KATHY: Mookie?

MOOKIE: Don't come back.

CAMERON: Another time.

KATHY: At least let me clean that scratch up for you.

(Kathy turns away from Cameron and Mookie in order to get the first aid kit from the kitchen cabinet. Mookie attacks Cameron. Cameron kicks Mookie. Kathy turns around with the first aid kit as Cameron is kicking Mookie.)

KATHY: Cameron, What are you doing? He's only a frightened cat.

MOOKIE: (Runs behind Kathy) Verbal abuse…physical abuse… I shouldn't be mistreated in my own home.

CAMERON: You and your cat together are a little weird for me.

KATHY: Why did you come over here?

CAMERON: You invited me. Remember?

KATHY: I invited you for… You've got the wrong girl.

MOOKIE: You've got the wrong girl.

CAMERON: Do yourself a favor. You're never gonna get a man unless you ditch that crazy cat.

(Kathy opens the door. Cameron exits. Kathy sits on the sofa holding Mookie.)

MOOKIE: Love is love and mean is mean. He was mean, Kathy. You and I deserve better.

KATHY: Still hungry. Time for takeout Asian Fusion.

MOOKIE: Yes! That delivery guy…he's a nice man. You should give him a chance Kathy.

KATHY: Love comes when you're not looking or maybe when you're looking. I looked behind those garbage pails and found love. I found you.

MOOKIE: I'm going to curl up next to you, baby.

KATHY: *How do I love thee?*

(Mookie & Kathy recite the poem with a spoken word style. Lights fade.)

MOOKIE & KATHY: Let me count the ways. I love thee...

(Lights Out)

End of Play

Her higher education at the Grace Institute for Vibration, her Master's Degree (mastery of self), was the only education she valued of her many accomplishments: MD, PhD, JD, EdD, MBA, and MDIV. Sondra credited the Institute for saving her life. She found in her studies at Grace the ecstasy she had longed for since she became femphysically aware. Spiritual connection with her clitoris, labia major, and labia minor was always present, always would be, forever and ever… Amen.

Acknowledgments

Theatre belongs in public spaces. Junelle Carter Bowman, manager of the George Bruce Library in Harlem, New York City, believed theatre should welcome everyone. Talented artists transformed these plays from the page to the stage for enthusiastic audiences. We became part of a historically rich tradition of art and community engagement. Actors who were members of Actors Equity Association performed courtesy of the union. I'm grateful to all:

Elizabeth Acosta, Segun Akande, Tonia Anderson, April Armstrong, Gregory Bastien, James Edward Becton, Lu Bellini, Sara Berg, Alex Blade Silver, Phillip Burke, Laurabeth Breya, Soraya Broukhim, Jordan Brown, Don Castro, Kim Chinh, Shamira Clark, Sabrina Colie, Ashlee Danielle, Billy Davis, Charles Duke, Jose Febus, Michael Flood, Lawrence Floyd, Sidiki Fofana (RIP), Jeannine Foster McKelvia, Nimo Ghandhi, Keith Gittens, Bryan Henao, Mike Hodge (RIP), Fulton Hodges, Mary Hodges, Denise Alessandria Hurd, Sean Kenin, Ariel Kim, Justin Lord, Rachel Lu, Julie Ann Lucas, Sharron Lynn (RIP), Jamil Mangan, Tom Martin, Alisha May, Kellie Mc Cants, Isreal McKinney Scott, Harry Miller, Ivan Moore, Khemali Murray (RIP), Marie Elena O'Brien, Ashton Pena, Beverly Prentice Campbell, Clea Rivera, Betsy Rosen, Krystal Seli, Tracy Shar, Norman Anthony Small, LeVera Sutton, Althea Alexis Vyfhuis, Douglas Wade, William Oliver Watkins, David D. Wright, and Gameela Wright.

I'm grateful for our community partners: Articulation NY LLC, ART MOVEZ, Brooklyn Savvy, Ideacoil, Jacob Restaurant, Lrg Enterprises, Wines by Mozel, and Sister's Uptown Bookstore & Cultural Center.

And when we couldn't commune with each other for live performance, Short Plays to Nourish the Mind & Soul have been enjoyed as literature. Celeste Rita Baker provided priceless feedback. My mother Florence Davidson and sister Cheryl showered me with encouragement. Many thanks to the phenomenal team at Aqueduct Press; L. Timmel Duchamp, Tom Duchamp, and Kath Wilham. Once again, I'm honored to have my work recognized and published in their prestigious Conversations Pieces series.

About the Author

Dr. Cesi Davidson is a New York based writer. Cesi is the author of four anthologies of plays, numerous theatrical compositions, and works of non-fiction. She travels everywhere she wants with her imagination. It's her honor to be a storyteller. Cesi is grateful to be lovingly surrounded by her partner, adult children, family, and friends who support her freedom to write without boundaries.

Short Plays to Nourish
the Mind & Soul Series

Articulation, 2019

Fricatives, 2021

Bilabials, 2022